SAMANTHA SPINNER
AND THE
SUPER-SECRET PLANS

SAMANTHA SPINNER
AND THE SUPER-SECRET PLANS

RUSSELL GINNS

ILLUSTRATED BY BARBARA FISINGER

DELACORTE PRESS

Text copyright © 2018 by Russell Ginns
Jacket and interior illustrations copyright © 2018 by Barbara Fisinger

Image Credits: Florida Center for Instructional Technology, pp. 83 (bottom), 159 (both), 221; public domain pp. 96, 116 (bottom), 126 (bottom); SewerHistory.org p. 126 (top); Shutterstock, Inc. pp. 1, 52, 83, (top), 101, 116 (top), 190

Visit us on the Web! rhcbooks.com

Educators and librarians, for a variety of teaching tools, visit us at RHTeachersLibrarians.com

Library of Congress Cataloging-in-Publication Data
Names: Ginns, Russell, author.
Title: Samantha Spinner and the super-secret plans / Russell Ginns.
Description: First edition. | New York: Delacorte Press [2018] | Summary: Samantha's uncle mysteriously disappears, leaving behind extravagant gifts for her siblings and an old, rusty, red umbrella for Samantha that may contain clues to his whereabouts.
Identifiers: LCCN 2016058798 | ISBN 978-1-5247-2000-1 (hc) |
ISBN 978-1-5247-2001-8 (glb) | ISBN 978-1-5247-2002-5 (el)
Subjects: | CYAC: Missing persons—Fiction. | Uncles—Fiction. | Family life—Fiction. | Adventure and adventurers—Fiction. | Mystery and detective stories.
Classification: LCC PZ7.G438943 Sam 2018 | DDC [Fic]—dc23

The text of this book is set in 13.7-point Galena.
Interior design by Stephanie Moss

Printed in the United States of America
10 9 8 7 6 5 4 3 2 1
First Edition

Random House Children's Books supports the First Amendment and celebrates the right to read.

TO KELLY SCHRUM

This book happened because of you.
Other great things continue to happen because of you.

The Eiffel Tower

The Eiffel Tower stands in the heart of Paris, France. Built for a world's fair, it was completed in 1889. At 1,063 feet high, it's the tallest building in the city. For more than forty years, it was the tallest building in the world.

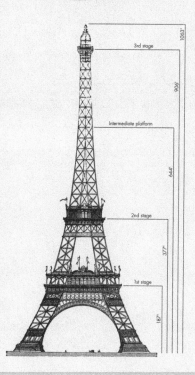

Every year, millions of visitors ride the elevator to the top and gaze upon the beautiful city of Paris.

The tower is made out of huge iron beams connected by metal fasteners called *rivets*. There are more than 2.5 million rivets holding the massive structure together.

* * *

One of the rivets isn't a rivet at all, but a button. Look for it two feet up on a large support beam at the northeast corner of the first platform. It stands out from the other rivets because it is shiny silver and not painted brown.

Press it and you'll hear a soft, low hum. After sixty seconds, a hatch will open, revealing a ladder stretching the length of the support beam.

Enter and descend. The pull of air will become stronger as you climb down. You may let go at any time. Before you hit the ground, you'll be sucked into a pneumatic tube.

CHAPTER ONE

UNEXPLAINED VANISHING PERSON

Samantha went searching for Uncle Paul.

Nobody had seen him for days.

On Friday morning, he'd made strawberry waffles and helped everyone get ready for the day. He reminded Buffy to include her books and pencils in the large handbag she lugged to school. Then he waited for the bus with Samantha and Nipper, and he walked their pug, Dennis, to the park and back. After he dropped Dennis at home, he shuffled across the driveway in his bright orange flip-flops to his one-room apartment above the garage.

That was the last anyone had heard or seen of him.

When she looked for him on Saturday, Samantha figured he was at the flea market, where he traded snow

3

globes and souvenirs every weekend. But she couldn't find him then, or on Sunday, either. So on Sunday evening she went up the stairs and peeked through his apartment door. His crates of books, magnets, stickers, and maps were stacked neatly against the wall, but there was no sign of him anywhere.

On Monday morning, he didn't show up to make breakfast. That was when the whole Spinner family agreed that Uncle Paul was officially missing.

Two police officers came to investigate, and Samantha's dad lent them an extra-powerful flashlight. They seemed a lot more interested in the experimental high-candlepower lightbulb than anything they shined it on in Uncle Paul's apartment.

They returned to the Spinners' kitchen after a five-minute search.

"We didn't see anything out of the ordinary," one officer told them. "We can't say for certain that he's dead."

"Dead?" all five Spinners asked at the same time.

"Well, there's always a chance that he's alive somewhere," said the other officer.

As he spoke, he picked up two apples from the kitchen counter and juggled them absentmindedly with one hand.

"Sometimes uncles just go missing without telling anyone," he said, and put the apples back on the counter.

They promised to fill out an Unexplained Vanishing Person Form and left.

Soon after that, Mrs. Spinner headed off to the North Seattle Animal Hospital, where she was Director of Rodent and Lizard Care. Mr. Spinner left for the American Institute of Lamps, where he was Senior Lightbulb Tester. And Buffy, forgetting her books and pencils, grabbed her giant handbag and walked to school.

For the first time in years, Samantha and her brother, Nipper, waited by themselves for the bus.

Of course, Samantha knew that Uncle Paul would never *just go missing* without telling anyone, especially her. She knew something was deeply wrong, but she had no idea what to do about a missing uncle. So when the bus pulled up, she climbed on board and went to school.

That afternoon, all three kids gathered under the basketball net hanging outside their uncle's apartment.

"Last week, I showed Uncle Paul *this* new hat and *this* new handbag," said Buffy. She held them up as evidence for Samantha and Nipper to examine.

"Usually he'd make a joke about how I need a five-hundred-and-fifty-room mansion for all my accessories," she recalled with a sigh. "But he didn't tease me at all. Maybe he knew he was doomed."

"Maybe he was kidnapped," said Nipper. "Maybe he exploded."

Buffy thought about that and looked around.

"If he did, then where are all the blown-up pieces of hideous orange shoes?" she asked.

Samantha was pretty sure Uncle Paul hadn't exploded. Her brother and sister were exactly as helpful as she expected them to be—not much at all. She left them standing under the basketball net and headed down the block to Volunteer Park.

In the center of the park, an art museum overlooked the city, with a view of downtown Seattle and the Olympic Mountains far in the distance. Uncle Paul spent a lot of time at that museum, so Samantha hoped she might get some help from Olivia Turtle, head of museum security.

When Samantha told her about Uncle Paul's disappearance, Olivia seemed worried, too. Unfortunately, not for the same reasons as Samantha.

"So he just went . . . missing?" Olivia asked slowly.

Samantha nodded.

"Well, I hope you find him, young lady," she said. "There's a big convention here next month, and security guards are coming from all over the world. I was going to ask your uncle to be on my trivia quiz team."

She adjusted her badge.

"Nobody knows about art and architecture like Pajama Paul," she said.

It always bothered Samantha when people called her uncle Pajama Paul. True, he did walk around in green plaid pajamas and a pair of bright orange flip-flops all day every day. She had never seen him wearing anything else.

But there was so much more to Paul Spinner than plaid pajamas.

Every night, he would sit with Samantha and Nipper on the stairs to his apartment above the garage, and tell stories about amazing places all over the world. He talked about the Great Wall of China and a mountain city called Machu Picchu. He talked about what it would have been like to travel on the *Titanic*.

He knew an awful lot about cathedrals and fountains and faraway countries, especially for someone who wore green plaid pajamas and bright orange flip-flops all day every day.

He'd taught Samantha how to say "Please," "Where is the tallest building in the city?" and "Thank you" in eleven languages.

Every now and then, he'd come back from the flea market with something interesting and give it to Nipper. Last year, he'd given Nipper an old postage stamp with a picture of an upside-down airplane on it. Nipper took it to school on a windy day and it blew away during recess.

Buffy made it clear that she didn't want anything from the flea market. Nothing involving fleas of any kind was welcome in her life.

Paul didn't bring items for Samantha, either. Instead, he'd always bring her a story or a riddle or an amazing fact about the world.

Sometimes she'd even help him find things to collect and trade.

Samantha spent the next several days looking for secret magnets or stickers left behind by her uncle to let her know he was all right, or that he was thinking about her. She looked everywhere in the house and around the neighborhood. She found nothing.

After a week, Samantha's parents finally let her investigate the apartment above the garage. She led Nipper and Dennis up the stairs, and the three of them sniffed around.

The sofa bed was closed up neatly. Dozens of books about everything from ancient weapons to scuba diving filled one tall bookcase. There were also a lot of books about travel and languages. The two wooden crates Uncle Paul carried to the flea market each Saturday were full of his usual collections.

Samantha and Nipper sifted through the stacks of license plates and brochures. They recognized most of it. Uncle Paul had shown it to them many times.

Samantha inspected her uncle's prized trophy, which rested on a coffee table in the middle of the room. Two years earlier, Uncle Paul had taken a trip to Washington, DC, and won second place in a hula hoop contest by keeping his hoop going for twenty-two hours. The winner was a trained monkey that twirled its hips for twenty-two hours and five minutes. Some people thought Uncle Paul should have claimed victory and demanded the first-place trophy. The competition was only supposed to be open to humans. But he seemed quite happy with second place—as if it were his first choice.

Dennis sniffed the second-place trophy. He licked it a few times and trotted away.

Samantha and Nipper noticed a piece of paper pinned to the wall opposite the windows.

```
I HOPE
YOUR   DAD
MAKES A LOT OF
WAFFLES  FOR  YOU
```

Samantha examined the note up close.

"What could this possibly mean?" she said.

"It means that Dad's going to have to step up and become the new breakfast maker," said Nipper.

Both kids stared at the note. They read the first letter of each word. They read it backward. They read it forward. They looked for numbers hidden somewhere on the page that might reveal a secret code. Nope. There was nothing they could make of the odd message.

Samantha and Nipper spent the rest of the afternoon searching the apartment, but they couldn't find any clues. Uncle Paul hadn't left a phone number or an address anywhere. There was nothing special or mysterious hidden behind the sofa or under the rug. Just the note on the wall.

That evening, Samantha's parents called everyone into the kitchen for a family meeting.

"Join us here, you three," said their dad, who sat next to their mother at the table. He held what looked to be a handwritten letter in one hand. In his other hand he held one of the experimental lighting gadgets he often brought home from work.

"When you told me about the note you found in Uncle Paul's apartment, I decided to look around the kitchen," their mother said. "Your father's been struggling to make oatmeal and toast all week, so he never went near the waffle iron. It turns out this letter was hidden under it the whole time."

"It seemed like an unwise electrical decision," said their father. "Let's adjust the color balance of the light." He tilted the pages and the glowing self-powered bulb at different angles.

"We really should view this with a high-candlepower light source and the most accurate shade of—"

Mrs. Spinner lifted the letter from her husband's fingers and began to read out loud.

"Dear Buffy, Sam, and Nipper. By the time you read this, I'll be gone. But don't think I haven't loved getting to know all three of you. I'm sure by now your parents spilled the beans that I'm an explorer and one of very few people who know about the Super-Secret—

"I don't believe this one bit," Buffy interrupted.

"What a bunch of hooey!" added Nipper.

Mrs. Spinner pointed two fingers at Buffy and Nipper and made eye contact. As a veterinarian, she had a lot of experience getting anxious chinchillas and chameleons to keep still while she bandaged their toes or un-peanut-buttered their tails. Getting children to settle down came easily to her.

Samantha waited patiently.

"Now, where was I?" their mom asked, and continued reading.

> *"You kids are probably thinking that this is all a bunch of hooey, but it's a big secret I've kept for a long time . . . for my safety, for your parents' safety, and for your safety, too."*

The letter was five pages long, and in it Uncle Paul explained that he was one of the richest people in the history of the world. He didn't do a very good job of detailing where all the money came from. He mentioned underwater treasure and something about gold bars. The story was confusing.

Samantha sat quietly as her mother read page after page. Uncle Paul ended by repeating how much he loved his nieces and nephew and saying that he didn't want them to be sad that he was gone.

"'Don't start feeling too bad, kids,'" their mother read, "'because it's time for the grown-ups to break out some big presents.'"

The kids all stopped breathing for a second. They sat at the table in silence. Nipper looked at Samantha. Samantha glanced sideways at Buffy. Buffy used her compact to inspect her lipstick, but she was really looking at her brother and sister in the tiny mirror. All three of the Spinner children were trying to play it cool, pretending they hadn't heard the words "big presents."

Mrs. Spinner put down the letter and handed Buffy an envelope. Eagerly, Buffy tore it open. Inside, she found a check made out to her for $2,400,000,000. A note was attached to it with a paper clip.

Have fun shopping.

—Uncle Paul

Mrs. Spinner looked at her husband. "Where did this money come from?" she asked, not really expecting him to know.

Mr. Spinner shrugged. "I didn't think Paul had a job," he said as he handed a folder to Nipper.

Nipper opened it to find a packet of papers. He read the top sheet. It was the deed to Yankee Stadium. All the baseball players' contracts were attached to the deed with a binder clip. Nipper closed the folder to read the note that was taped to the front.

Don't miss opening day.
—Uncle Paul

"That might be a warning not to lose these, Nipper," Mrs. Spinner said, tapping the folder.

"Yeah. Like that old superhero comic book you fed to the birds," said Buffy. "And everything else Uncle Paul gives you."

"I didn't feed it to anyone," said Nipper. "A pigeon flew away with it while I was tying my shoe."

"Uncle Paul always says if nobody lost anything, nothing would be valuable," Samantha reminded her family. She had waited patiently. Now it was her turn.

For a moment, her parents glanced at each other without saying anything. Then her dad reached under the table and lifted up a red umbrella. He handed it to her quietly.

It was old and worn. A paper tag dangled from the wooden handle. The tag had a message, too.

Watch out for the RAIN.
—Uncle Paul

Samantha stared at the umbrella.

Her uncle had given her an umbrella. A rusty old umbrella.

"Don't worry," said Mrs. Spinner. "I'm pretty sure we can figure out how all this crazy, mixed-up stuff fits together."

Samantha was pretty sure of one thing already: *It wasn't fair!*

It really wasn't fair.

In her heart, she knew that if anyone ever wrote a book about her life, the title of Chapter Two would be "It Wasn't Fair."

CHAPTER TWO

IT WASN'T FAIR

Samantha's brother's real name was Jeremy Bernard Spinner, but everyone called him Nipper. That was because when he was little, he used to bite people all the time. Never hard enough to break the skin, but it sure hurt! Now he was eight, and he didn't do that very much anymore. Actually, it had been three years, seven months, and twelve days since he'd bitten anyone. Everyone still called him Nipper.

With his very own baseball stadium and professional ball club, Nipper was looking forward to the best summer ever. He might even be getting an awesome magical ring on his finger—a World Series ring!

Meanwhile, Samantha's older sister, Buffy, was already having the time of her life. As soon as she deposited the check for $2,400,000,000 in her bank account, she rode her bike to her favorite boutique in Seattle and bought the fanciest, most expensive handbag she could find. She went back to the store an hour later in a cab and bought an even larger handbag to carry the first one in. Then she returned in a stretch limo and bought the store. A great, grand shopping spree had begun.

Buffy headed to the mall early Saturday afternoon and came back home five hours later with a convoy of tractor-trailers. Each truck was filled with scarves and sunglasses.

"When is this going to stop?" Nipper shouted to Samantha.

"I can't hear you," she replied, looking down at the umbrella.

Big rigs rolled past them for the rest of the day, dumping crates of accessories in the backyard.

Sunday was all about sweaters and belts. A fresh column of trucks rumbled down the Spinners' narrow side drive, and crews added the cargo to the rising pile of crates, which was now almost as tall as the Spinner house itself.

There was no school that Monday because it was parent-teacher day. So Buffy woke up and started shopping all over again. For decades to come, that day would be remembered as Shoe Day in malls and department stores throughout the Pacific Northwest.

Wearing her most expensive scarf and designer sunglasses, Buffy went to every shop within twenty-five miles of Seattle and systematically purchased every pump, sneaker, and boot in sizes 9-1/2 and 10. Meanwhile, a squad of foot proxies—teenagers with the same size and shape feet as Buffy's—visited stores in all the major cities of Oregon, Idaho, and Washington State, buying footwear on her behalf.

By Tuesday morning, Buffy's wardrobe was as fabulous as it was ever going to be. So she shifted gears. She announced that her destiny was to be a movie star and that she had set her sights on Hollywood.

Mr. and Mrs. Spinner said it was fine that Buffy wanted to become an actress but that she absolutely could not leave school.

Buffy listened to her parents and agreed she wouldn't leave school. She paid for a team of engineers to raise Lake Union High School, including its football field, parking lot, and flagpole, onto a caravan of two dozen massive flatbed trucks, and she took the school with her. Students, teachers, books, band instruments, cafeteria food, and all began the journey south.

They left behind an empty dirt field, a row of lockers that were permanently rusted shut, and a girl named

Nelly McPepper, who Buffy refused to bring because she wore white after Labor Day.

No one heard from Buffy for two weeks. Then, one afternoon while Samantha was moping in the living room, Nipper walked in waving an envelope.

"Mom just gave me this letter to share with you," he said.

The envelope was addressed in ornate calligraphy drawn with gold ink. It was from Scarlett Hydrangea, in Beverly Hills, California. There was at least ninety-seven dollars in stamps on it.

"Who the heck is Scarlett Hydrangea?" asked Nipper.

Samantha opened the letter and read it out loud.

"Dearest Sammy and Little Nipper,
  I'm the star of my own big-budget movie, and it's going to be a blockbuster. No one seems impressed yet, but once I learn my lines, I know that the world will appreciate my brilliance.
  My 550-room mansion is delightful. Uncle Paul was right—I finally have space for all my accessories! I even have space for both of you when you come to visit. There are two empty stalls in the stable behind my waterfall. I'm planning to keep a pair of rainbow unicorns there, but no one has been able to find any for

me to buy yet. Come soon and you are welcome to them. (The stalls, not the unicorns.)

Write back, but please don't rattle on about your boring lives!

Kisses,
Scarlett Hydrangea

PS: That's my new stage name."

"Okay. Got it," said Nipper.

Samantha dropped the letter on the floor. "I'm just like poor Nelly McPepper," she moaned, and flopped facedown on the couch. "I have nothing to do and nowhere to go."

Nipper was about to point out that she could go to California and stay in Buffy's stable, when Dennis trotted in. Samantha looked up from where she lay to see that the dog had a shiny new collar. A gold band sparkled with colorful gems ranging in size from tiny rubies to a huge blue diamond about the size of a walnut. Uncle Paul had even left a fabulous present for their dog!

"Even *you* got something amazing!" she said to the pug.

Dennis stepped forward and sniffed Samantha's hand, but she didn't move. He was getting petted a lot less often lately.

Since Uncle Paul had disappeared, power moping now took the place of petting, and just about everything else, for Samantha. Come to think of it, other than going to school, doing homework, and snooping for signs of Uncle Paul, lying around feeling blue had become her main activity.

For weeks, Samantha kept hoping that there was something more to the rusty old umbrella. She inspected it several times a day. Maybe there was a key to a secret bank vault hidden inside the handle. There wasn't. She peeked through a tiny hole in the cloth near the center. Nope, there was nothing to see. The whole rickety thing seemed like it was about to fall apart. She fiddled with it over and over again and finally gave up.

Uncle Paul had taught Samantha about archaeology and how to ride a bike. Samantha had helped him solve puzzles and found interesting stickers and buttons for his collections. On the day before he disappeared, she gave him a set of scratch-and-sniff stickers that smelled like fruit.

"You know, Samantha, people can remember smells two hundred and fifty times better than sights or sounds," he'd told her. "Smells have the power to unlock important memories."

He scratched at one of the stickers.

"*Berry* important," he said.

If memories were so important, then why did Uncle Paul forget about her? Why would he just go missing without telling her? And how could he give her silly big sister all that money and her brother a major-league baseball team and give her nothing more than a piece of junk and a note about the weather?

The fact remained: it wasn't fair.

Samantha looked at Nipper. He was still standing there, waiting for her to say "Watch out for the rain."

"Watch out for the *rain*," she said gloomily, and rested her head back down on a cushion. Samantha had begun to mutter the phrase to everyone several times every day.

With that out of the way, Nipper turned to leave. His thoughts were on his franchise.

The Spinners lived in Seattle, but his parents had promised that the whole family could take a trip to see his Yankees in New York City as soon as school ended. It might even help Samantha focus a little bit less on her moping.

"Cheer up," said Nipper as he crossed the living room. "You can sit with me in the owner's box. Sooner or later there are going to be some rain delays, and that old umbrella will come in handy."

He left her, walked through the kitchen, and grabbed his folder full of contracts from the counter. Then he headed outside to see if any friends, neighbors, utility workers, or passersby were around to hear more about his baseball team.

CHAPTER THREE

NO BACKSIES

The Spinners had two of the worst next-door neighbors on planet Earth.

On the south side of their house was Morgan Bogan Bogden-Loople, a boy who never, ever said anything that wasn't ridiculous or impossible. When Samantha went looking for clues about Uncle Paul, she asked Morgan Bogan if he had seen him.

"I saw your missing uncle just a few minutes ago," he told her confidently. "He was wearing big rubber boots and said he was on his way to take cello lessons. He had a pet raccoon on his shoulder."

Their other neighbor was Missy Snoddgrass. She lived next door to the Spinners on the north side, closer to the park. She was a little girl with curly blond hair, freckles, and a cute button nose. She was Double-Triple-Super Evil.

When Nipper walked out of his house and hopped the bushes that afternoon, with a folder full of papers to show Missy that he owned the New York Yankees, he should have known he was in for trouble.

"My uncle disappeared," he told Missy as she stared at him through the screen door at the side of her house.

"I know all about that," she said.

"Now I'm the new owner of Yankee Stadium!" Nipper said, excited to share the news with someone who seemed to care. He held up a fancy certificate with a big gold seal on it. "This is the official deed to the ballpark." He flashed it for her to see.

Missy pushed open the door and slid out onto the landing a few feet from Nipper.

"Impressive," she said, looking directly into his eyes without blinking. She did not sound very impressed.

"I've got contracts for all the players, too," he added cheerfully.

Missy rubbed her chin with her right hand. Then she extended that hand toward Nipper, palm up.

"Fascinating. You should let me see some of those contracts."

Nipper opened his folder and handed her several pages stapled together.

"Here," he said, beaming with pride.

Missy inspected the pages carefully. He watched her lips move silently as she read the fine print.

Finally, she looked up from the contract and smiled at him. There was a huge gap where she was missing a tooth.

"He's one of the finest pitchers in the entire American League," she told him. "Uniquely talented. Will you let me see one of the outfielders?"

Nipper thumbed through his folder and held up another contract. Missy took the papers from him and read them more quickly.

"Amazing," she concluded. "Now can I see the document for the stadium?"

At last, Nipper had found someone interested in his Yankees. For weeks, he had tried to engage Samantha in conversations about baseballs, stadiums, Leagues, the infield fly rule, hot dogs, or even big, fuzzy mascots. Nothing he said could distract her from the moping. She just wanted to whine about the umbrella. Of course, Nipper was the first to admit that he understood nothing about big sisters—or any eleven-year-old girl, for that matter.

Soon he had handed the complete set of documents to his neighbor.

"Well, I think we both know the secret to a winning sports team," she said. Suddenly she started speaking in a very soft whisper. "It's the players that you *trade*. Don't you agree?"

"What was that last part?" asked Nipper.

"I said 'trade.' Don't you agree?" she said clearly.

"Sure," he answered cheerfully.

"Terrific," Missy announced. She reached into her back pocket and took out a large magnifying glass. It had a shiny metal band around the lens and a blue handle.

Nipper thought she was going to use it to examine the papers again. Instead, she gave it to him.

"What's this?" he asked, taking it from her.

"That's what some people refer to as a *hand lens*," she explained. "Of course, you can still call it a magnifying glass. I don't mind at all. It's yours now. And no backsies!"

"Backsies?" asked Nipper, confused. He turned the hand lens over. The blue plastic handle was flimsy. It had a crack at the bottom. "I don't understand."

Missy reached into the front pocket of her yellow polka-dot blouse and took out several pages torn from a book. She shuffled through them quickly and handed one to Nipper.

It came from a dictionary. He read it out loud.

"No backsies:
noun phrase.
[nō bak-seez]
A command used to prevent a return action or consequence. This term originates from the game of tag, stopping players from immediately tagging the player who tagged them. More broadly, it prevents someone from going back on an agreement or trade."

"I didn't want an agreement . . . or a trade," said Nipper, beginning to feel very nervous. "And I don't like this magnifying glass."

"Didn't you hear me call it a hand lens?" Missy corrected him. "Well, you will definitely learn to love it. Bye."

She tucked all the papers under one arm and turned to open the screen door.

"Wait!" shouted Nipper, reaching out to grab her sleeve.

Missy spun around violently and shook a fist two inches from his nose.

"Never touch me again or I will smash you like a bug. Endless misery and woe will fall upon you like the rain!"

Nipper could swear he saw her eyes flash red with fury. Then she smiled and looked down at her watch.

"Whoopsy. Look at the time," she chirped happily, and stepped back into her house, slamming the door behind her.

And with that, she was gone.

And so were his New York Yankees.

Nipper was going to miss Opening Day.

Nipper stood on Missy's porch for a few minutes. Then he slunk down the stairs and backed away from the Snoddgrass driveway. A magical new ring wasn't in his future, and he didn't feel like jumping over the bushes anymore. Soon he was inside his house, stomping up the stairs toward the second floor.

"Sam!" he called. "I lost my baseball team!"

CHAPTER FOUR

FRIDAY MORNING

All the people were gone.

Dennis sat under the table.

When the Man with the Orange Shoes first showed up, a waffle fell on the floor.

There was syrup and there was powdered sugar.

It could happen again.

Something went *hiss*.

Dennis looked around.

He didn't see anything.

He didn't smell anything.

Someday, he would get another waffle.

CHAPTER FIVE

FRIDAY AFTERNOON

For weeks, Samantha divided her moping evenly between flopping on the living room sofa, sulking at the kitchen table during meals, and muttering to herself as she paced under the basketball net outside Uncle Paul's apartment. Every afternoon, she took Dennis for a walk around the neighborhood. She spent half of each walk looking for clues about Uncle Paul and why he had disappeared and the other half wondering why he'd done it without saying goodbye.

When the weather was bad, however, she stayed indoors to power mope. There, she'd lie on the floor and write depressing entries in her journal. It was springtime in Seattle, so it rained for a few hours almost every day. The little black notebook already had sixteen sad entries.

On the thirty-fifth afternoon since Uncle Paul had gone missing, Samantha chose her bedroom for the gloom session. She invited her brother to join her. Ever since he'd lost his Yankees, Nipper was more than willing to mope along with her.

Samantha was on the floor, lying on her back with her feet on the bed. She flipped through her journal to one of the recent entries and read out loud.

> "There's a little bit of Nelly McPepper in all of us.
>
> One moment, the future looks great. The next moment, all our hopes and dreams are jacked up onto a massive flatbed truck rolling south.
>
> Life's a bumpy ride, McPeppered with potholes that fling us, filled with despair, into the air. It's so unfair! And there's no umbrella big enough to shield us from the daily drizzle of our dreary lives.
>
> We have nothing to do and nowhere to go."

Nipper half ignored her. He was looking at an old baseball card Uncle Paul had given him.

"Honus Wagner," Nipper said, using the magnifying glass to examine the stats on the back. "A guy who never got to play with the New York Yankees . . . just like me."

"Wait," said Samantha. "Let me take a closer look at that card."

Nipper had already put it away and was examining the pencils, paper clips, and coins on Samantha's desk.

"Sam, did you ever see an old penny up close? There's a man sitting between the pillars of the building."

"That's Abraham Lincoln," said Samantha. "The building is the Lincoln Memorial."

Peering through the glass, he moved toward her.

"Let me peek inside your nose."

"Cut it out," Samantha said, and pushed him away.

Nipper tripped and fell. He landed flat on his back, still holding the magnifier in front of his face. He started to study the underside of the desk.

"Hey. I remember this piece of gum. I stuck it here last year. Do you think it has any flavor left?"

"You are *exceptionally* gross," said Samantha. "And stop touching my things."

"Technically, that gum is one of *my* things," said Nipper.

He rolled onto his side and started examining objects on the floor.

"There's a neat pattern on the bottom of your

sandals." He lifted a flap on the old umbrella. "This has a cool pattern inside, too."

He squinted at the inside of the umbrella for a few seconds. Then he stopped. He sat up quickly.

"Come here, Sam. I want you to see something."

"Nipper. I do not want to see a shoe or a bug or inside your ear."

"No, really." He handed her the magnifying glass. "Use this."

He pushed the button on the worn wooden handle and the umbrella popped open.

"Hey! Close it!" Samantha shouted. "The last thing I need is more bad luck."

"Just look."

Samantha took the magnifying glass and lay down on her back under the open umbrella with her brother. She squinted to focus on what she was seeing, and, to her surprise, Nipper was right. There *was* a pattern on the inside of the umbrella. There were lines and shapes everywhere. But it was more than that. She took a closer look at things and saw that there were tiny pictures. Hundreds of them. No, thousands. She could see buildings, streets, tunnels, towers, ladders, stairs, trees, bridges, and fountains.

The umbrella was a map!

She recognized some of the drawings. There was the

Eiffel Tower. There was the White House. There was a castle, an elephant, an ear of corn. But there were many more things that weren't familiar at all.

Samantha was pretty sure that one big shape was China and another was Australia. She could make out the Taj Mahal and the Leaning Tower of Pisa . . . and everything was connected!

There were lines and arrows running from one picture to another. It looked like there was a tunnel under the Washington Monument. A zigzaggy line ran from the Statue of Liberty to a big sunken boat in the North Atlantic Ocean.

The umbrella was more than a map. It was some kind of top-secret blueprint of the whole world.

"Nipper," Samantha whispered excitedly, "I think Uncle Paul gave me super-secret plans."

The Hope Diamond

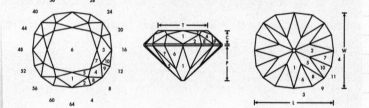

The Hope Diamond is a 45-carat blue diamond about the size of a walnut.

A French merchant obtained it from a mine in India and first put it on display in the 1600s. Since then, it has become one of the most treasured and storied gems in the world.

Blue diamonds are extremely rare. Only about one in one hundred thousand diamonds is brightly colored, and blue is one of the rarest colors. A *huge* blue diamond is incredibly rare.

Since 1958, the Hope Diamond has been on display at the Smithsonian National Museum of Natural History in Washington, DC.

It is said to be insured for a value of $250,000,000.

* * *

The huge diamond on display at the Smithsonian, surrounded by armed guards and a very elaborate security system, is actually a replica. It is a blue piece of glass that has a street value of seventy-five cents.

The real gem was stolen from the museum several years ago.

A tiny radio transmitter is attached to the true Hope Diamond. It emits a continuous signal broadcasting the gem's whereabouts. Anyone with a receiver tuned to the correct frequency can pinpoint the location of the precious gem once they get within a few miles.

CHAPTER SIX

I SEE LONDON, I SEE FRANCE

Normally, Nipper was not the first person Samantha would want anywhere near her while she investigated an amazing discovery. Yet there they were, spending the rest of that day together on their hands and knees, poring over drawings and details on an upside-down umbrella.

At first, they passed the magnifying glass back and forth, examining the tiny illustrations. They took turns calling out anything they could recognize.

"Alaska," announced Samantha. She passed the magnifying glass to her brother.

"I think I see pyramids," Nipper countered.

"The Hollywood sign," Samantha fired back.

"Not fair," said Nipper. "The Hollywood sign has letters. It's like its own big label."

Most of the illustrations, however, did not have any letters or labels. The complete umbrella lining was an octagonal snarl of drawings with lines and arrows that ran in every direction, from one picture to another. There were a few numbers here and there and a few random words.

It was as if someone had taken an atlas, a dictionary, and a few board games; chopped them up in a blender; and splattered all the tiny bits inside the umbrella.

What Samantha and Nipper were *really* looking for was a picture or clue connected to Seattle. If they could find anything in their hometown, then they would be able to go and investigate.

They'd have proof that the Plans were what they thought they were.

Then maybe, Samantha thought, this might lead to a clue about what happened to Uncle Paul!

Unfortunately, after several hours of inspection, they'd found nothing related to their home in the Pacific Northwest.

By the time they came downstairs for dinner that night, both kids had lost a bit of their enthusiasm.

"What have you been doing, you two?" asked their dad.

"Research," said Nipper.

"He's helping me with research for a story I'm writing," added Samantha quickly.

She wasn't ready to tell her parents about the new discovery. If Uncle Paul had kept it secret, maybe it was important for her and Nipper to keep it secret, too.

"Well, that sounds like a fine project," said their mother. "And it's good to hear that you're writing something other than those gloomy notes in that little black journal."

Samantha and Nipper ate slowly and quietly. Staring at fabric for hours at a time would make almost anyone feel drowsy.

As soon as they finished, Samantha and Nipper decided to make another trip across the driveway and up the stairs to Uncle Paul's apartment. It gave them a break from staring at the inside of an umbrella. But it didn't give them any new clues.

Samantha read the spine of every book on the shelves.

Nipper studied the note pinned to the wall opposite the windows.

"I still think there's some clue here about Uncle Paul and where he went," he said, and tapped on the word *waffles* with an index finger. Then he took a step back and squinted at the arrangement of words to see if it was shaped like an umbrella. It wasn't.

Samantha looked over at the hula hoop trophy on

the coffee table and then out the window to their house across the driveway. It was getting dark outside and starting to rain.

"Come on," she said. "Let's go back to the Plans."

They stepped quickly through the drizzle, down the wooden stairs and across the driveway, and went through the kitchen and headed up the stairs and into Samantha's bedroom. Then they got down on their hands and knees and resumed searching, squinting, and passing the magnifying glass back and forth.

Samantha studied a zigzaggy line that started at one edge of the umbrella. She traced it with her finger across the fabric. It ran through a blob shaped like a mitten.

"Michigan," she said, and continued tracing the line. It ran through a jagged shape that looked like the letter Y.

"Mozambique, maybe," she continued, sounding uncertain. "And . . . and . . . ," she continued as the line neared the center of the umbrella.

"And what?" asked Nipper.

"And . . . nothing. I got nothing," she answered.

Nipper let out a big sigh. "I'm more than tired of this," he said, and grabbed the magnifying glass.

He flipped the umbrella over and started to inspect the outside.

"There's nothing to see," said Samantha. "Just red fabric."

Nipper continued to look though the magnifying glass, then stopped at a spot near the center of the umbrella. He looked up at Samantha.

"Red fabric . . . and a flying saucer!" he said loudly.

"What are you talking about?" she asked.

"See for yourself," he said, handing the magnifying glass back to her.

Samantha stared through the lens and examined the umbrella. She noticed the tiny hole that she had peeked through a dozen times from the inside. Beside it, on the outside, she saw what Nipper saw.

There really was a little drawing of a flying saucer. It was just above the hole, and it looked very familiar.

"I was right, wasn't I?" Nipper asked.

"Hang on," said Samantha.

She took a closer look. The flying saucer, drawn on a tiny bit of fabric, was poking out next to the hole.

Samantha folded the little bit of cloth back with a finger. She rubbed it a few times so it would stay in place. Then she carefully turned the umbrella over and started searching to find the same spot on the inside.

Nipper leaned in and looked over her shoulder through the magnifying glass.

There was a slender three-legged tower with the tiny flying saucer at the top.

"The Space Needle," they both said at the same time.

Anyone who has been to Seattle knows the Space Needle. It's a giant tower with a flying saucer–shaped top, and it stands in the north end of the city. On foggy days, all you can see is the top and its blinking red light, so it looks like space aliens are flying over the city.

Uncle Paul had poked a hole in the umbrella right at that spot. Right where they lived!

Samantha shifted the lens around, inspecting the drawings nearby. To the left of the Space Needle she saw a drawing

of a mailbox. It had the number 3 written on it. To the right of the mailbox, there was a round building with arched windows.

She and Nipper looked at each other, then back at the drawing. It was the brick water tower at the south end of Volunteer Park—just three houses down from where the Spinners lived.

"That's it, Sam!" Nipper shouted. "That's our corner!"

"And I bet that's our mailbox," Samantha added, pointing at the little drawing.

"We've got to check this out *now,*" said Nipper, scrambling to his feet. "I'm heading out there."

Samantha rose quickly, reached for the back of his shirt, and grabbed him before he could get away. It was nearly midnight, raining, and pitch-black outside.

"First thing in the morning," she insisted.

Then she let go of her brother's shirt and picked up the umbrella. She folded it with a little more care than before.

That night, she slept with the umbrella propped against the wall, right beside her bed.

CHAPTER SEVEN

EXPOS AND EXPEDITIONS

Early Saturday morning, Samantha's parents were getting ready for the EPE—the Exotic Pet Expo—in Tacoma. It was an all-day event, so they didn't expect to be home until evening. Mrs. Spinner was going to deliver her popular lecture "Nutrition for Extremely Large Lizards." Mr. Spinner was going along to check out the very latest in light-up dog toys.

They were bringing Dennis with them. Pets were always welcome on the EPE exhibit floor. Just not in the food court.

"Be good, you two," their father told Samantha and Nipper as he carried lunches and a spare umbrella to the car. "Don't break anything while we're gone."

Both kids knew he meant lamps and lightbulbs when he said that.

"And, Nipper," their mother added, "you really should stay away from that Snoddgrass girl. She's not very nice to you."

Neither parent said anything about not going out and investigating a secret map to landmarks all over the world—which is exactly what Samantha and Nipper were planning to do.

As the car pulled away down the drive, Samantha noticed Dennis through the rear window. His bejeweled collar sparkled in the sun. He had a weird expression on his face, as if he was hearing a strange noise. Or maybe he was just thinking about squirrels or waffles.

The car turned and disappeared down the street. Samantha and Nipper sprang into action. They had at least eight hours until their parents would return, and this was their chance to see if the Plans were real. Within minutes, they were out the door.

They hurried past the Snoddgrass lair, then past two more houses, and reached the end of the block.

A blue mailbox stood at the corner of Prospect Street and Thirteenth Avenue.

Samantha and Nipper had walked past it hundreds of times. And just like this time, there didn't seem to be anything special about it.

They both stared at the metal box with the round top. A label on the front said "US Mail." There was a faded chalk drawing on the sidewalk of a kid with a sword through his head. Nipper had been there when Missy Snoddgrass drew that a few days ago. She'd ordered him to act it out, but he ran away.

"What exactly are we looking for?" Nipper asked.

"I haven't the foggiest idea," Samantha said, and shrugged.

She walked slowly around the mailbox, looking for anything unusual. When she'd completed her circle, she opened the umbrella and gestured to her brother.

"Help me look," she said.

Nipper took out the magnifying glass and raised it to the umbrella. Together, they examined the little drawing of the mailbox with the number 3 written on it.

Samantha closed the umbrella, and they began to search the mailbox for buttons or a lever or anything unusual. Then they looked for anything that said "3." They found nothing.

Samantha reached out and pulled down on the handle of the mailbox flap. The opening was at her eye level, so she peeked inside.

"Nothing," she said, squinting into the dark. "It's just a regular old mailbox."

"Let me have a look," said Nipper, pushing her out of the way and standing on tiptoe.

Momentarily the same height as his big sister, he peered into the mailbox slot as well and saw . . . nothing.

"I told you there wasn't anything to see," said Samantha, holding the flap open and gesturing at it with her other hand.

She let the mailbox close and something deep inside made a loud metal click. Samantha and Nipper looked at each other. A whirring noise kicked in.

Sister and brother jumped back, sure that something was about to happen. They stood on the sidewalk and watched the mailbox carefully.

"Did you break it?" asked Nipper.

"No," said Samantha. "But I think I know what the number three means."

She stepped forward and grabbed the handle again, pulling the flap down and holding it open for at least ten seconds before letting go. She did this twice, and, each time, a click and a whirr followed. Then she hopped backward to stand beside her brother on the sidewalk.

There was a rumbling, clanking noise, as if something very heavy was being unlocked. Then they heard a loud hiss and felt a gust of air rushing past them. With a low mechanical murmur, the ground beneath the mailbox moved. A section of pavement with the mailbox on top rose out of the ground, revealing a large rectangular shape underneath.

"It's a super-secret porta-potty!" said Nipper.

Samantha chose to ignore him. She leaned forward carefully.

There was an opening on the face of the steel chamber, with a long stairway leading down below the street.

Both kids peered down along the stairway to where it disappeared. Then Nipper tapped Samantha on the shoulder and pointed up to some bright yellow letters stenciled above the opening:

MAGTRAIN

"Magtrain? What could that possibly mean?" Samantha asked.

Nipper held out his hands, palms up. "I haven't the foggiest idea," he said, and shrugged.

Samantha folded the umbrella and slung it over her shoulder.

"You look like a soldier," said Nipper.

Samantha smiled.

"Nope," she said, moving toward the opening. "I'm an explorer, like Uncle Paul. Now let's go find him."

Nipper followed her through the opening. They disappeared beneath the raised mailbox as they marched one after the other down the stairs.

The VHSR Plan

In 1906, the scientist Robert Goddard published an article about the possibility of "Very High Speed Railways" running beneath the surface of the earth.

He described how a network of underground tunnels partnered with magnetically propelled trains (magtrains) could transport people across the country at extremely high speeds.

Harnessing the opposing forces of magnets, a magtrain would float above its track, eliminating friction, and thus would be able to race from city to city faster than any airplane could travel. Magtrains might travel at speeds greater than 10,000 miles per hour, reducing the travel time between California and New York to a mere fifteen minutes.

This article, of course, was only a theoretical study. People often talk about plans to build supersonic trains called Underground Jet Networks or Hyperloops.

So far, no one has ever announced the completion of a Very High Speed Transit system.

* * *

There is a hidden magtrain station in Seattle. It is located near Volunteer Park, about two miles from downtown. The entrance is below an ordinary-looking mailbox across from the brick water tower.

Grasp the handle of the mailbox door and open it all the way. Hold it open for at least ten seconds, or until you hear the motor engage, before you let it close. Repeat this two more times. The ground beneath the mailbox will rise slowly, revealing a staircase.

Wait until the mailbox has risen completely. You will hear a loud clicking sound indicating that the chamber has locked into position. Then it is safe to walk down the stairs.

You will reach an elaborately decorated chamber. This is a secret station with many tunnels. Each one leads to a different destination around the globe.

CHAPTER EIGHT

LOCATION, LOCATION, LOCATION

Samantha and Nipper reached the bottom of the stairs and found themselves in the center of a round room. Light trickled in from the opening behind them and from storm drains running along Prospect Street above. There was enough light for them to find their way around the space, but it was too dim to see most of the details of the room.

They surveyed the chamber. Stone archways surrounded them. Each one appeared to be the entrance to a dark tunnel.

"Is this some sort of station?" Samantha asked.

"Seven, eight, nine," said Nipper, counting the openings. "If you count the one that came from the street."

As their eyes adjusted to the room, they could make out words chiseled over each arch in huge letters. There was just enough light to read the names. Both kids squinted at the words:

DYNAMITE
PARIS
BARABOO
DUCK
ZZYZX
EDFU
WAGGA WAGGA
WAHOO
EXIT

"Baraboo?" Samantha asked. "Zzyzx?"

"This is all very, very clear," said Nipper.

Of course it wasn't, and both kids stood silently in the center of the round room, puzzling over the meaning of the words.

"Well, we came in through an exit . . . and we've certainly heard of Paris," Samantha said carefully. "But are all of these really places? They seem like a bunch of funny words."

"What's funnier," her brother asked, "Wagga Wagga or Wahoo?"

"That's not my point," she said. "I was just expecting every tunnel to lead us to a city or a famous landmark or— Wait a minute."

Samantha remembered a road trip the family had taken last winter. They'd driven to the Pacific Pandemonium amusement park near Spokane, Washington. They were most of the way there when they stopped at a place called Dynamite. They'd picked up Uncle Paul, who was visiting a flea market.

Samantha asked her uncle what kind of flea market would set up in the middle of nowhere.

"No place is in the middle of nowhere," he answered.

Before she could ask Uncle Paul anything else, Nipper kicked her in the shin by accident. He had been accidentally kicking her since they left Seattle. That was 275 miles of continuous accidental kicking. She exploded in a rage, and then all three Spinner kids screamed at each other for the rest of the ride to the amusement park.

But Dynamite *was* the name of a place.

"I think these really are locations," she told Nipper as she gestured up at the arches.

"Then we are definitely going to Wahoo," he said with certainty. "That sounds like the kind of place where—"

"No," Samantha said firmly. "It's my umbrella . . . and we . . . are going . . . to Paris."

CHAPTER NINE

CHARGE!

Samantha and Nipper stepped through the "Paris" arch-
way and walked along the corridor. There was enough
light for them to see their feet, but not much more. She
guessed, from the sound of their footsteps, that they
were probably walking on a tiled floor.

As she walked, she looked up and squinted, trying
to make out what the ceiling above them looked like.
Then Nipper whacked her with an outstretched arm,
and she stopped.

"Look down," he said.

They'd reached a ledge.

Light filtered down through a grate in the ceiling, so
she could make out the details below. About three feet
down from the ledge, two wide metal tracks led off into

the distance and disappeared into the darkness. And on the tracks, directly below Samantha and Nipper, sat a small open car. The strange vehicle looked like something that belonged on a roller coaster.

"Magtrain," said Nipper.

Samantha thought again about their family trip to Pacific Pandemonium. The visit had been cut short after Nipper insisted that Samantha sit next to him on the Holy-cow-a-bunga! roller coaster over and over again. After four times around the winding, flipping, twisting track, Samantha had had enough and got off. Nipper stayed on and rode the Holy-cow-a-bunga! nine more times. Then he barfed mightily and the staff had to close the attraction while they cleaned out the car. The Spinners left the park right after that.

Everyone in the family was extremely grouchy that their trip to the amusement park was cut short, but Samantha remembered having fun the whole ride home guessing license plate messages with Uncle Paul.

"C-L-W-N-C-four-R," she said, reading the plate on a tiny red sedan in front of them.

"Clown car!" Uncle Paul answered quickly.

A van sped past them. As it went by, they saw LVFR4NC3 on the plate.

"Love France!" she called out.

"Or *leave* France," her uncle said thoughtfully.

Looking down at the magtrain car, Samantha guessed

it was about the same size as the one they rode on the Holy-cow-a-bunga! But it looked odd, even for a roller-coaster car. There were benches wide enough for two riders in the front and in the back. They were connected by a single bucket seat in the middle, so there was room for a total of five passengers. Viewed from the top, the car was shaped like a big letter H.

"Shotgun!" shouted Nipper as he bolted ahead of Samantha, hopped over the ledge, and plopped onto the right side of the front bench. He rapped his knuckles against the wide, curved windshield that stretched across the front of the car. Then he waved, signaling her to join him.

Samantha was never, ever going to sit next to her brother on any ride again if she could help it. She hopped down from the ledge. Then she took a big step forward and lowered herself into the bucket seat in the center of the H. They both sat for a minute, looking around and waiting for something to happen.

Samantha noticed a glowing red oval button on the back of the bench in front of her.

She reached out and pressed it.

The button clicked down and a soft hum began to fill the air. The oval turned yellow and numbers and letters appeared across its front.

OOOOOO MPH

The tiny hairs on her arms stood up, and from where she sat Samantha could see the tracks begin to glow. They bathed the chamber all around them with soft orange light.

In front of her, Nipper's hair stuck out in all directions. Illuminated by the glowing tracks, his head looked like a porcupine. She could feel the hair on her head sticking out, too.

"Electric," said Nipper.

The hum grew louder and the car began to move forward. Samantha quickly stowed the umbrella in a narrow space below her feet and gripped the sides of her seat. She prepared herself for a roller-coaster ride.

But there was no jolt of g-force. The car began to speed up, slowly and incredibly smoothly. Samantha looked down at the oval. The numbers were rising, and they were already moving pretty fast.

```
000003 MPH
000008 MPH
000090 MPH
```

"Magnetic," said Nipper.

Samantha kept her eyes on the oval and watched the numbers advance. She could feel the car continuing to accelerate.

Suddenly Samantha understood the word *magtrain*. They were floating above the tracks, propelled by magnets.

The rails beneath the train now glowed bright yellow, so Samantha could clearly see the walls around her and Nipper—and that they were racing past them very quickly. The numbers in the center of the oval kept shooting upward.

```
000140 MPH
000308 MPH
000912 MPH
001200 MPH
```

"Fantastic!" Nipper shouted.

He turned to look back at her and carefully stood up from the bench. The air blasting over the windshield whipped his hair around wildly.

She smiled at her brother. This *was* pretty fun.

A card of some sort slipped out of Nipper's pocket and was caught by the rushing air. Samantha and Nipper both followed its fluttering path onto the tracks and watched it vanish into the long tunnel behind them.

"Sam!" Nipper shouted. "I lost my old baseball card!"

Samantha shook her head but didn't say anything. He was going to lose that card sooner or later.

The walls narrowed and Nipper sat back down. The car was moving faster and faster. They rocketed smoothly down an endless tunnel. The rails were now bright white.

Samantha glanced at the yellow oval.

010000 MPH

"We've stopped accelerating," she called. "It's about five thousand miles from Seattle to Paris," she added. "We should be there in thirty minutes."

"That depends," her brother shouted. "Which way around the earth are we going?"

Samantha had to admit that it wasn't a completely ridiculous question. It was one she might have been able to answer if she'd noted which way they were pointing when they took off below the surface of the planet. But it had been hard to see much of anything in the little round station room. They probably missed a lot of details there. The magtrain coasted on and on and on. Considering how fast they were going, the ride was pretty comfortable.

As they raced through the tunnel, Samantha took out her little black journal and opened it to the most recent entry. Yesterday, she was planning to add to it. Then Nipper interrupted her—and they'd discovered the Plans.

She reread the sad sentences.

> *There's a little bit of Nelly McPepper hidden inside all of us. It's a tiny egg of sadness, waiting to hatch into a giant chicken of woe. The sky is gloomy and gray because the sun has been jacked up on a massive flatbed truck rolling south. We stand soaking in the dreary drizzle each rainy day, clueless fools in a crummy cruel world.*
>
> *We have nothing to do and nowhere to go.*

Samantha could hear the motors of the magtrain car purring like a giant electronic cat. She scratched out the gloomy lines and started over.

There is a hidden magtrain station in Seattle, Washington. It is located near Volunteer Park, about two miles from downtown. . . .

CHAPTER TEN

BAGUETTE ME NOT

Samantha looked up from her journal. The magtrain had come to a stop. It happened so smoothly that she hadn't noticed. Nipper was already standing on the platform outside the car, waving at her impatiently.

"Come on, Sam. Let's-go-let's-go!"

She put away her notebook. Then she grabbed the umbrella and climbed out onto the platform, next to her brother. The rails under the magtrain car still softly glowed orange, dimly lighting their surroundings. They were in a square chamber. The floor was paved with large stone tiles of different geometric shapes. Samantha had a feeling they were still underground.

"Mental note," she said to Nipper. She tapped her forehead. "Next time, we bring a flashlight."

"'Yes, you two,'" he responded, imitating their father. "'And make sure it's a high-candlepower light source.'"

"'With just the right color balance,'" Samantha added.

She gazed around the room. Behind them was the mouth of the train tunnel, but there didn't seem to be any other exits.

Nipper watched her.

"I looked everywhere while you were still writing," he said. "I can't find any way out of here."

"Let's check the Plans," said Samantha.

She swung the umbrella from over her shoulder and pressed the latch on the handle with her thumb. The red octagon burst open above her head.

"Magnifier, please," she said, extending her free hand toward her brother.

Samantha turned the open umbrella upside down and carefully placed it on the tiles, then crouched over it. Squinting in the dim light, she scanned the lining. She found the mailbox and the Space Needle. She picked a dotted line and followed it until it reached a shape that looked like a bunny, or maybe a rat. That clearly wasn't Paris or France. She started over and followed a line until it reached a little drawing of a circus tent. There was nothing that seemed French or Parisian about it. She went back to the Space Needle and picked another line.

She followed the new dotted line with her finger and traced a long path to one edge of the umbrella. The line stopped at a shape she thought she recognized.

"France?" she asked herself out loud.

Then she noticed that right beside it was a little drawing she recognized for sure: the Eiffel Tower.

"France," she answered herself out loud.

Inside the France shape was a square. Inside the square was a drawing of a shoe. On the shoe was the number 4.

Nipper leaned in and looked at the drawing. Then, puzzled, he looked at Samantha.

Samantha closed the umbrella and gazed at the floor. In the dim light, the tiled surface was a jumble of gray and black shapes. Triangles, rectangles, hexagons, and— Aha! About five feet from where she stood, she spotted a lone square.

She walked forward and stopped in the center of the tile.

"Stand here with me," she told Nipper.

He skipped over and hopped into the square. He bumped into his sister and she glared at him. He shifted a few inches away from her, but he stayed within the square.

"Okay, now what?" he asked.

Samantha thought about the drawing on the umbrella—the square, the shoe, and the number 4. This one was easy.

"One, two, three, four," she counted, stamping her foot each time.

There was a scraping noise overhead and a bright shaft of light enveloped them. A square hole had opened in the ceiling. As if powered by a huge spring, the tile they were standing on launched upward.

Samantha and Nipper reached toward each other and took hold. They hugged as the tile shot up toward the opening. With a loud click, the tile fit into the square hole . . . and they were outside!

They let go of each other immediately. Then they looked around.

Samantha and Nipper stood on one of a thousand stone tiles that made up a vast plaza. Around them, crowds of people milled about. Some of them wore matching T-shirts. Others had big, bulky backpacks. They were tourists from all over the world, chattering to each other in a dozen different languages. They snapped pictures of themselves, each other, and the glass pyramid that towered seventy feet over the courtyard.

A person dressed as a circus clown stood in a clearing, performing tricks for the passing tourists.

"I know this place," said Samantha. "We're outside France's most famous museum. That pyramid is the entrance to the Louvre."

"Did you say 'loo-ver'?" asked Nipper.

"No. It's 'Loo-vruh,'" Samantha said in slow, careful French. "It has some of the greatest treasures of the art world inside, including the *Mona Lisa* by Leonardo da Vinci."

"How do you know that?" asked Nipper.

"Uncle Paul told me about it," said Samantha. "You were there, too, but maybe you weren't listening carefully, like I was."

She thought about her missing uncle for a moment. "Actually, he mentioned this exact place a bunch of times," she said slowly.

Nipper wasn't listening carefully to her either, at the moment. He was looking around the crowded plaza.

"Sam," he said. "Nobody noticed us. We just popped out of a hole in the ground, and no one cares at all."

Samantha looked around, too.

"Well, people don't always notice amazing things right in front of their noses," she said. "Other stuff seems important, so they forget to take a closer look at—"

"Hold on," said Nipper. "There's something in front of *my* nose right now. Something that smells great. And I'm hungry."

Samantha sniffed twice and nodded in agreement. Something did smell wonderful.

Nipper began to push his way across the crowded plaza, following the scent. Samantha walked quickly after him, weaving around people. She followed her brother to a low stone wall that appeared to surround the plaza, then through a break in it. On the sidewalk a few yards away, a man stood beside a bright yellow food cart. The front half of the vehicle was a rectangular box balanced on two wheels. The back half was a bicycle. A metal rack rose from the front, supporting a red-and-white-striped awning. A dozen loaves of bread lined the shelves of the box. Some were long and thin, and others were wide. They smelled absolutely delicious.

Samantha caught up with Nipper and approached the man. He was wearing jeans, a black T-shirt, and a yellow apron. Stenciled on the sides of the cart and on his apron were large letters: *PAIN DU JOUR.*

Nipper waved at him, then sniffed the air dramatically and shook his head from side to side. Then he did it five more times. It reminded Samantha of Dennis.

As soon as Nipper had the man's attention, he called out cheerfully, "Sir. We don't want any pain, but could you give us some of that great bread?"

The man stared at him for a moment. Then he smiled.

"Not 'pain.' It's pronounced 'pan.' That is the French

word for *bread*," he explained in English, with a hint of a French accent.

Samantha glared at Nipper but didn't say anything. She wasn't sure if goofball kid brothers were as common in France as they were in the USA.

Nipper kept going. "Mr. Pan—or may I call you Peter? I'd like your freshest jumbo breadstick." He gestured toward Samantha. "My personal assistant will handle the finances."

"It is a baguette," said the vendor patiently. He grabbed one of the vertical loaves and slid it into a paper sleeve. Then he turned and held it out to Samantha. "Please pay two euros for your boss, young personal assistant lady."

There were so many things wrong with this exchange between her brother and the vendor that Samantha was speechless. And, unfortunately, euro-less.

She shrugged and held out both hands, palms up, to indicate that she had no money. Then she remembered that she did have some of the loose change from her desk. She quickly fished around in her pockets and came up with two quarters. Sheepishly, she presented them to the vendor.

Uncle Paul had taught her to say three things in eleven languages. The first thing was "please."

"*S'il vous plaît,*" she said carefully.

A look of disappointment washed over the man's face. He pulled the baguette away and put it back on display. Then he turned and opened a side door of the cart. He fumbled around inside for a moment and produced a different loaf of bread. It was already wrapped in paper.

"My half-dollar special for two special customers," he said. He handed the baguette to Samantha with one hand while taking the two quarters with the other.

Samantha eyed the delicious-smelling baguette on the shelf as she accepted the special bread. She unwrapped and examined it quickly. It felt a little hard and it didn't smell very fresh.

"When did you bake this?" she asked.

"Why . . . it was baked in the morning," said the man, sounding insulted.

"Which morning?" Samantha pressed.

Meanwhile, Nipper noticed a new scent. It was quite different from the aroma of freshly baked bread and it was absolutely not delicious. It smelled like old banana peels, melted crayons, and sweaty sneakers left in a backpack for a month.

"This is definitely not a freshly baked baguette," Samantha continued, arguing with the street vendor. As she spoke, she waved the bread in the air.

Nipper, nose twitching, was watching his sister when something flashed through the air and—*thwack!*—

hit the baguette. It sliced into the bread, coming to a stop halfway through the narrow loaf.

If it had actually been a freshly baked baguette, the sharp object would have sliced all the way through a light and flaky crust and out the other side. It would have continued in a straight line until it hit Samantha right between the eyes . . . and that would have been the end of this story.

Fortunately, it had been fifty-seven hours since the baker removed the special baguette from his oven and left it to cool. For that reason, the flying object remained lodged in the stale French bread.

"What's this?" asked Samantha, pulling the metal object from the bread and holding it up. It flashed silver in the light.

"It's a *shuriken*!" gasped Nipper. "A ninja throwing star!"

The flat, shiny object was indeed shaped like a star, about three inches across. It had eight needle-sharp points. The outline of a crown and two crossed swords was engraved in the center.

Samantha puzzled over the weapon and its engraving for a second. Then she slid it carefully into the front pocket of her pants.

Thwack! Bang!

A second flying blade whizzed at her and hit the bread. And a third sailed past Samantha's neck and slammed into the side of the bakery cart.

Alarmed, the vendor hopped onto his bicycle and began to pedal away.

Nipper grabbed a thick, round loaf off the back of the cart as the man departed, and he whirled around, holding the loaf in front of his face for protection.

Thunk! Thunk!

The round loaves were heavier and thicker than baguettes. Just in time, Nipper's bread stopped two metal stars from hitting his face.

"Sam! We're under attack!" he shouted to his sister.

The food cart was gone and they had walked too far

from the Louvre plaza to call for help. They were alone on the sidewalk, with nowhere to hide.

Halfway down the block, a hooded figure clad all in black tiptoed toward them. He may have thought that he was being sneaky, but his horrible smell gave him away.

With nothing but bread to defend themselves, the Spinners stood and faced the approaching menace.

CHAPTER ELEVEN

HIT THE ROAD, JERK

Samantha and Nipper had no formal martial arts training, but they had almost ten thousand hours of pillow-fighting experience between them. They had no idea why they were under attack, but they were not going down without a fight.

As the man drew close, they could see that he was indeed some kind of ninja. At least, he was dressed like one. He wore a black hood that covered his entire face, except for the narrowest slit where his eyes peeked through. He had on a long black coat and baggy black pants that drew tight around his shins, revealing black socks and black split-toe ninja slippers.

And he was smeared with garbage. Or that was what it looked like. Brown and green splotches covered his shirt and coat. A yellowish stripe ran down his left thigh. It looked like a bird had recently pooped on his right shoulder.

He moved swiftly and silently, but his smell screamed out loudly. In seconds, he was within a few feet of the kids. Then he stopped.

"How did you get that umbrella?" he demanded. "There are twenty ninjas in the United States right now, looking for—"

Nipper sprang forward. He moved quickly and maneuvered himself directly behind the shrouded man. Then, holding tight to his loaf of bread, he swung at the ninja's back with all his might.

There was a loud *thwack*. The bread struck something flat and hard beneath the ninja's shirt. It felt to Nipper almost like he'd hit a plank of wood.

In a flash, the ninja turned, drawing a long silver sword from a sheath at his side. Even faster than Nipper had launched himself, the ninja diced the bread into tiny cubes that dropped to the sidewalk. Before Nipper could react, the ninja raised one of his smelly feet and kicked him in the center of his chest, knocking him backward onto the bread cube–sprinkled pavement.

Samantha stepped between Nipper and their attacker. Defiantly, she held up the throwing star–studded baguette in one hand. In the other, she grasped the metal tip of the umbrella and pointed the wooden handle at him.

"I've heard that Parisians aren't friendly to visitors," she said. "But this is ridiculous."

"Yeah," said Nipper, scrambling back to his feet. "France isn't making a good first impression."

"I don't care about France," the ninja muttered. His accent might have been British. It was hard to tell, as it was coming through the filthy face mask. It clearly wasn't a French accent. He shifted his body, adjusting whatever it was that he was concealing inside his shirt. Then he lifted his sword and waved it at Samantha. "Hand it over," he told her.

"You don't want this bread," said Samantha. "It's stale. And it's full of metal blades."

"No!" said the man in black, much louder. "The umbrella."

"You forgot to say *s'il vous plaît*," said Samantha.

"I don't speak French," said the ninja. "Now let me have it."

Samantha was happy to let him have it. She gathered her strength and brought the umbrella down on his head as hard as she could.

Wham! The man let go of his sword and fell face-first onto the pavement, knocked out cold.

Nipper bent down and rapped his knuckles on the

center of the unconscious ninja's back. It was like knocking on a door. He started to reach for the ninja's sword, but Samantha grabbed his shoulder.

"Leave it," she said. "The handle's gross and sticky, and we've got to get out of here *now*."

Nipper looked back at the grimy man and his grimy weapon and nodded in agreement. Then he and his sister ran.

They retraced their path along the sidewalk and through the break in the stone wall and headed into the crowded Louvre plaza. They pushed their way through the tourists, searching for the spot on the ground where they'd emerged. Just as they were about to reach the huge glass pyramid, they stopped short. Two ninjas stood, side by side, in their path, and it looked like they were on the very tile that had lifted Samantha and her brother from the magtrain chamber. The two black-clad figures didn't notice the kids. They were busy studying the tile beneath their feet. They knew it wasn't just an ordinary part of the plaza. They were clearly trying to figure out how to make it do something.

"They found the square," said Nipper. "But I don't think they know about the secret stomp."

Samantha glanced sideways to make sure that she still had the umbrella on her shoulder. Then she grabbed her brother's hand and they ran through the crowd and away from the Louvre. They turned to their right and ran to the closest point of the low stone wall that surrounded the plaza. They hopped over it and sat down on the grass, out of sight.

"I think I saw another way out of here," Samantha said, catching her breath.

She popped open the umbrella and Nipper handed her the magnifying glass.

"Right here," she said, pointing at the drawing of the Eiffel Tower centered in the lens. "I think there's some kind of connection from here to Italy."

There was a tiny arrow beside the lowest landing of the Eiffel Tower, just above the arch that forms the legs. Above the arrow, tiny dots were arranged in a cluster that looked like the letter R. A line started there and ran halfway across the umbrella. Unlike the dotted magtrain line that ran from Seattle to France, this line was a chain of little spirals. It looked to Samantha like a gust of wind.

The line ended at a picture that was definitely the boot-shaped country, Italy.

"There must be a lot of ways to get around using the Plans," Samantha said. "Now let's go find that boot— I mean, those dots," she said. "Or that letter R. Or an arrow, or, um—"

"I get it, Sam," Nipper cut her off. "Let's go check out the tower."

They hopped back over the wall and quickly headed

away from the plaza. They ran down a narrow street lined with restaurants and small hotels and didn't stop until they came to a gloomy-looking woman standing next to a table and chairs outside a café.

Samantha had remembered that the Eiffel Tower was Paris's tallest building, so she was ready with the second thing Uncle Paul had taught her to say in French: "Where is the tallest building in Paris?"

"*Où se trouve le plus grand édifice de Paris?*" she asked.

The woman's expression brightened instantly. "*La Tour Eiffel!*" she exclaimed, and pointed down the street. She gestured with a curved hand to show that they should follow the bend in the road ahead.

Samantha said, "*Merci.*" That was the third and final thing she knew how to say in French.

She and Nipper ran down the street, and as they rounded the curve, they saw the banks of the river Seine. Off in the distance, the Eiffel Tower came into view.

The Louvre

The Louvre is an immense, sprawling palace in Paris, France. It displays thirty-five thousand works of art and houses hundreds of thousands more. It is one of the world's largest museums.

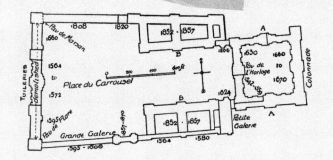

It was originally a fortress and then a royal palace. For more than two hundred years, it has been France's great public art museum.

The Louvre has been expanded many times. Today, its most prominent feature is a giant glass pyramid surrounded on three sides by different wings of the building.

Each year, almost ten million visitors come to see Leonardo da Vinci's *Mona Lisa* and countless other works of art.

* * *

A secret transit station is located directly beneath the Louvre.

Look for a square tile about ten feet from the entrance to the giant glass pyramid. It is much larger than the thousands of other squares that pave the plaza, and big enough for up to four adults to stand on.

While you're in the center of the tile, stomp your foot four times. The tile will descend quickly, coming to a stop in the entrance chamber to the Paris magtrain station. A new tile will slide into place above your head.

To return to the surface, stomp four times again. The tile will rise and slide back into place. Chances are, no one will notice as you emerge in the museum's courtyard.

CHAPTER TWELVE

UP, DOWN, AND OUT

Samantha and Nipper jogged along the banks of the river Seine to the park with the Eiffel Tower standing near its northwestern end. As they made their way through the broad green expanse, Samantha took a moment to look around.

"I can't believe we're actually in Paris," she said to Nipper.

"Yeah," he replied. He looked back over his shoulder to see if any ninjas were behind them. "Let's get *out of* Paris as soon as we can."

Samantha felt a jab from the throwing star in her pocket. Nipper was right. They needed to get home safely and figure out what was going on.

"Are you eating something?" she asked him.

Nipper's mouth was full. He held out a handful of ninja-cut bread cubes he'd picked up from the sidewalk.

"Oh, yuck," she exclaimed.

"It's actually quite delicious," he mumbled as they continued running through the park.

Soon they reached the base of the tower. Visitors, tour guides, souvenir vendors, and street performers milled about the wide space between the four massive legs. A long line of people talked and snacked and snapped photos as they waited to ride the elevator to the top.

"Over there," Samantha said, pointing. "We're taking the stairs."

Nipper stopped in his tracks. He tilted his head back and stared up at the tower. It was over a thousand feet high. His arms fell limp at his sides.

"Relax," said Samantha. "We're only going up to the first landing."

Nipper counted the two platforms on the tower before it curved upward into the sky. Then he counted fourteen flights of stairs leading up to the first one.

"Okay," he said. "I guess it's better than being attacked by ninjas."

Samantha had to agree. She skirted the people in line for the elevator and headed for the stairs. There didn't seem to be anyone taking tickets just then, so they walked through the turnstile without stopping.

Side by side, they marched up the stairs.

Clang! Clang! Clang! The metal echoed under their feet as they climbed, zigging and zagging up the endless staircase. At each new landing, the many gaps between the rails and beams of the complex structure grew larger. Samantha and Nipper started to catch glimpses of the city below.

Flight after flight they rose, until they reached the first platform. As they stepped out onto it, the beautiful city of Paris unfolded beneath them. The river Seine surrounded them on three sides. To their right, they saw the distant spires of the grand cathedral, Notre-Dame de Paris, rising from an island in the middle of the Seine, and far off they could see the great avenue leading to the Arc de Triomphe, the giant stone victory arch.

They stood silent for a moment, taking in the glorious view and catching their breath from the long climb. As Samantha gazed down at the park below, she spotted a line of four black dots moving toward the base of the tower.

"Sightseeing tour's over," she told her brother. "Find the R."

Nipper nodded and they began inspecting the platform, winding their way around tourists, who surveyed the scene below.

Samantha scanned the beams that made up the

mighty tower. There were small round bumps on every surface—the rivets that held the structure together.

"Over here!" Nipper called. He stood beside one of the large, slanted girders that formed the tower's northernmost leg. He was pointing to a group of rivets at knee height on the painted metal surface.

Samantha looked to her left and right to see if any of the tourists were paying attention to her or her brother. No one had noticed them at all. Then she crossed the platform to investigate.

"R marks the spot," said Nipper.

All around the tower, rivets ran in straight lines and X-shaped patterns. In this one small area, however, about thirty rivets formed a large letter R. One rivet in the top corner of the cluster wasn't painted. Instead, it was shiny and silver.

Nipper was pointing at that very rivet. "I think it's a button," he said.

"Be careful," Samantha cautioned. "Before you press it, we should try to—"

Before she could finish, Nipper reached out with his index finger and pushed the button.

There was a loud click.

She started again: "We should try to figure out what—"

Several loud thumps came from deep inside the pillar.

"Never mind," she said.

A soft, low humming sound began. They waited for a little while. The hum continued, but nothing happened.

Nipper pushed the button again. This time, the humming stopped. He reached out once more and pushed the button. The click, thumps, and hum happened again. He pushed the button again and the noises stopped.

"Now it's my turn," Samantha announced, nudging her brother out of the way before he could get in another press.

Samantha pressed the button and they heard the same pattern of noises. Nipper was about to reach out and press the button again, but Samantha grabbed his finger.

"Can we please wait and see what happens?" she said, annoyed.

The hum continued. Samantha counted to ten and let go of Nipper's finger. They both waited while the sound went on for a full minute. Finally, it stopped, and there was a loud clunk and the sound of grinding gears. A panel in the girder swung out toward them like a refrigerator door.

Samantha looked around and was again surprised to see that no one else on the platform appeared to notice a thing. Everyone was simply too busy gazing out at the surrounding view of Paris to look at the Eiffel Tower itself.

Samantha turned back to the door and peered over her brother's shoulder into the opening. Inside was a hollow shaft, about four feet from side to side. It sloped down to the left at an angle that followed the tower's leg and disappeared out of sight. On the wall to the right of the door, a metal ladder ran up and down.

"Do you think we should just climb in?" Nipper asked. "Not that I'm scared, but, well, it's really dark in there."

Samantha opened her mouth to answer and a cloud of stink hit her. The scent of glue, moldy peanut butter, and a hundred uncapped whiteboard markers filled the air.

Samantha looked at Nipper. Hands over their noses, they ran to the staircase they'd just climbed and peered over the railing. Four figures dressed in black were making their way up the tower. They were only three flights away from where the Spinners stood on the first platform.

"I don't mind the dark so much," Nipper said quickly. He spun around and ran back toward the pillar.

Samantha followed him to the pillar and got there just as he hopped through the opening, grabbed the ladder, and began to descend, disappearing rapidly.

Samantha was right behind him. She paused for a moment to secure the umbrella over her shoulder. Then she stepped forward into the opening and grabbed a metal rung with both hands.

"Stop!" someone shouted. "Don't move."

Samantha couldn't help it. She turned around. She saw the same smelly ninja they'd encountered outside the Louvre just as he stepped onto the platform. And he was even filthier than before. He had a fresh layer of bread crumbs covering his front, from where he had fallen onto the sidewalk. Several wads of gum stuck to his shrouded face—including one big pink blob directly in the center of his forehead. The three other black-clad figures stood a few feet behind him, and they were just as dirty.

Her brother's voice drifted up from inside the shaft. "Are you still coming, Sam?"

The ninja looked past Samantha into the shaft beyond.

"Hey, boy! Is that you?" the crumb-and-gum-covered ninja shouted to Nipper. "Come back up here so we can finish that friendly chat we were having about—"

Samantha spotted a handle on the back of the iron door, grabbed it, and pulled the door shut as hard as she could. A loud clang reverberated up and down the shaft.

She was in the dark.

Samantha clung to the ladder in the silence. Suddenly there was a *tap-tap-tap*ping on the other side of the iron door. She stayed frozen, holding on tight to the metal rung, breathing out when it finally stopped. Then frantic pounding erupted. Then the pounding ended and the muffled sound of four really unhappy ninjas yelling at each other trickled into the chamber.

Samantha relaxed. "I think we're safe, Nipper," she called downward. "They saw the door, but I don't think they know about the secret button."

"Come on!" she heard her brother shout. "There's more light down here."

Carefully, Samantha reached out her toe until she felt the next rung under her foot. She moved one hand at a time and began to follow her brother down the slanted shaft.

As she descended, narrow slivers of light began to seep in through the edges of the structure, cutting through the darkness. Samantha could see the rungs of the ladder, and, far below, she saw her brother looking up, waiting for her. She could also feel a gentle breeze.

At first she thought air was coming through the same gaps as the light. As she continued, however, the breeze became stronger.

She stopped and shifted her shoulder to make sure her umbrella was secure. Then she resumed her downward climb.

"Sam," she heard her brother calling. "This is getting weirder."

He was about twenty feet below her. His hair was swirling around wildly.

As she moved toward her brother along the ladder, the breeze grew stronger with every step. It was so windy that gusts of air whipped Samantha's hair in front of her face; she had to move slower and with more care.

It was getting harder to hear, and it took more and more strength to stay on the ladder.

"Sam!" she heard Nipper shout over the sound of the rushing air. She was sure that he was only a few feet away.

She lowered herself down one more rung and felt her shoe press into something soft and handlike.

"Yow!" her brother screamed over the roar of the wind.

She looked down to see him yank his hand out from under her foot. Then his other hand slipped off the ladder. For a split second, she saw her brother's startled expression as he frantically looked up, hands out, desperately trying to grab on to something.

Then he was gone.

"Nipper!" Sam screamed.

She waited for a crash or a thump or some other terrible sound of an eight-year-old going *splat*.

But there was nothing. Just the roar of the gale-force winds that tugged at her like some giant, invisible vacuum cleaner. She clung to the ladder with all her might.

Her knuckles turned white as she strained to hang on. The shuriken slipped out of her front pocket. She heard it ricochet off a metal rung as it dropped away. She felt her journal slide slowly from her back pocket, but there was nothing she could do about it. Gone.

She felt the umbrella slipping off her shoulder and down her right arm. She took her left hand from the rung to try to shove the strap back in place. A gust of air yanked at her with such force that she couldn't hold on with just one hand.

And then she was airborne.

Helplessly, Samantha fell. The mighty suction pulled her downward so fast that the ladder and the walls of the shaft became a blur. She gritted her teeth and waited for impact.

And then her direction changed—and she was moving sideways!

It was getting brighter.

Curved walls shot past her on all sides. Every ten yards or so, a ring of lights flush with the walls flashed past. It took her a moment, but she realized she was rocketing through a giant pneumatic tube.

She heard the sound of ruffling pages, and some-

thing fluttered around her head. It was her journal! She snatched the book and shoved it back into her pocket.

Far ahead of her, she could see Nipper.

He waved to her with both hands as he zoomed along through the tube. In one hand, he held the ninja throwing star.

"Hey, Sam!" he shouted cheerfully. "I think you were right. I think we're on our way to Italy!"

The *Mona Lisa*

The best-known, most visited, most written-about portrait in the world is a painting of a smiling woman by Leonardo da Vinci.

It is an oil painting on a poplar wood panel. Most experts believe it is a picture of Lisa Gherardini, a woman who lived in Italy in the 1500s. Almost nothing else is known about her or her famous smile.

The *Mona Lisa* has been on permanent display in the Louvre Museum in Paris since 1797.

* * *

The directors of the Louvre have been covering up a secret for several years: someone stole the *Mona Lisa*.

Visitors who go to the famous museum to view the portrait are now staring at page 967 of *Famous Art You Should Know from Around the World*.

No one has any idea where the real painting is, or how thieves were able to break into the museum. There were no clues other than a terrible, terrible smell.

French authorities, art experts, and customs agents have been searching the globe for the original masterpiece for many years.

Every museum guard in the world secretly hopes to be the one who rescues the *Mona Lisa*.

CHAPTER THIRTEEN

UNDER WHERE?

Normally, Nipper was not the first person Samantha would want anywhere near her as she flew through a giant pneumatic tube. Yet there they were, sailing on a blast of pressurized air from France to Italy. Every now and then they bumped into each other.

"Watch out," said Samantha when his elbow glanced off her ear. But she knew there really wasn't much Nipper could do about it.

There also wasn't much to see inside the long tunnel, but it sure zoomed by fast!

Samantha wondered if Uncle Paul traveled by pneumatic tube. It didn't seem like a smart way to go, tumbling from place to place. And did he get chased from place to place, too?

The tube suddenly banked left and then right, and Samantha could feel herself slowing down. Then the tube curved up and over in a big loop-de-loop.

"Crazy straw!" shouted Nipper.

They did two more loops, and they slowed down a bit more each time. As the last of the pressurized air swirled around them, they tumbled out onto the floor of a small chamber, landing in a pile.

"Not as smooth as the magtrain," Samantha muttered as she untangled herself from her brother and got up off the floor. She spotted the umbrella and picked it up quickly.

Nipper hopped to his feet beside her and they looked around. They stood in the center of a narrow space, lit by torches on three of the four walls. The flickering light illuminated a checkerboard pattern in the large, square floor tiles.

"Here we go again," said Nipper. "Check the Plans and see how many steps or stomps or skips we have to do to unlock the secret exit."

Samantha walked to the large wooden door in front of them and turned the handle. She pushed the door open slowly and light flooded the room.

"That works, too," said Nipper, and he followed her outside.

They stepped out into a wide plaza surrounded by ornate buildings and towers. A cathedral with a gigantic eight-sided dome loomed over them.

Samantha recognized their location immediately. Night after night, Uncle Paul had talked about the Italian Renaissance, a time of great artists and architects. The huge terra-cotta-tiled dome was the top of the Duomo, the great Florence cathedral. They were standing in the historic center of Florence, Italy.

Samantha gazed up at a high structure next to the cathedral. It was a slender, square tower covered in white, green, and red marble and decorated with row upon row of arches, pillars, sculptures, and colorful shapes. She remembered her uncle looking upward and waving his hands happily as he described the bell tower.

Then she looked around the plaza. There were statues and fountains and, of course, visitors from around the world. Everyone was excited and looking up and down and sideways. Samantha could tell that many of them were having trouble deciding what to see first.

Nipper tapped her on the shoulder and held out the ninja throwing star.

"Get us home before more of these start flying at us," he said, and handed it to her.

Of the many places she'd heard about from Uncle Paul, Florence was high on the list of cities she'd hoped to visit one day. Now she was there—and she already had to leave!

"How long do you think we have until the ninjas get here?" asked Nipper.

"I don't know if they followed us," said Samantha. "And I'm not even sure how they found us in the first place."

She took the star from him and adjusted the umbrella on her shoulder. Then she led him into the narrow alley that ran between the Duomo and the bell tower. If there were ninjas around, she didn't want to draw their attention. She knelt down, opened the umbrella, took the magnifying glass from Nipper, and began to look for a way home.

She couldn't find any lines pointing to the mailbox in Seattle, but next to the little boot shape of Italy, she saw a letter *U* with the number 16 in its center.

A wavy line from the *U* led across the lining, back to the France shape, and connected with the dotted magtrain line.

"What could that possibly mean?" asked Nipper, kneeling and peering over her shoulder.

"Well, what starts with *U*?" she asked him.

"*Underwear,*" said Nipper quickly. Then he rubbed his chin and continued slowly. "*Unusual uncle . . . unexplained umbrella . . . uptown umpires, unfortunately unseen unless . . .*"

Samantha took a closer look at the letter U and noticed that there were four tiny white dots on each side.

"Hold on," she said. "It's a horseshoe."

"Okay," said Nipper, rising to his feet. "Let's go find a horse and kick it sixteen times, and—"

"Nipper!" she cut him off. "First, that's awful. And second, that's a horse's shoe, so maybe *you* get kicked sixteen times."

She stood up, closed the umbrella, and led him back onto the plaza.

They walked around the outside of the cathedral looking for a horse statue, or a horse painting, or even a real live horse.

They noticed a tall man standing on the steps of the Duomo, watching them closely.

"Leave this to me," said Nipper. He walked up to the man.

"Hay!" he shouted. He looked back at Samantha and winked. Then he started waving at the man and began to speak very loudly and slowly. "Is . . . there . . . a . . . horse . . . here?"

Expressionless, the man stared at him.

"Horsey? Yes?" Nipper continued. "Giddyap?" He held up his fists as if they were hooves. Then he began to prance around the man, stomping his feet in rhythm.

"Ne-heh-heh-hey! Ne-heh-heh-hey!" he whinnied, and shook his head from side to side while blowing loudly through his flapping lips.

Samantha grabbed her brother by the shoulder and stopped him.

"That's my brother," she said, rolling her eyes. "He wants to know if there is a horse nearby. Or maybe a statue of a horse."

"I know, young lady," the man said in English. "But that was hilarious!"

He chuckled, and pointed past them to a corner of the plaza.

"The Piazza della Signoria is that way," he said. "Very famous place, with very famous sculptures."

They gazed across the plaza. Many people were entering and exiting.

Samantha turned back toward the man.

"*Grazie,*" she said.

"*Prego,*" he replied, and nodded warmly.

Samantha and Nipper walked to the edge of the plaza and followed the throng. Couples holding hands, parents with kids, and tour groups in matching T-shirts all funneled into the street beyond.

"How did you know that guy spoke English?" Nipper asked as they moved with the crowd down the cobblestoned street.

"He was wearing a badge that said 'Museum Security,'" she answered. "He probably talks to visitors from around the world all day long."

Samantha thought about Olivia Turtle, the guard at the museum in Seattle. She could probably name all the statues in Florence. Just like Uncle Paul.

Five blocks later, the street opened onto a vast L-shaped plaza. Statues, vendors, and even more visitors filled the expanse. Samantha and Nipper stopped and gazed up at a stone fortress. It was a square, eight-story castle with a tall clock tower perched on top. Then they looked down again to the street and the entrance to the massive stone building.

Just to the left of the fortress door, they saw a huge white statue, almost twenty feet high. It was a young man, completely nude. He held a sling over his shoulder and looked off into the distance with a wary expression on his face.

"I know that one," said Nipper proudly. "That's David."

"Michelangelo's *David*," Samantha added.

Last year, Uncle Paul had given the Spinner family a magnet set. It included a magnet depicting the famous statue of the biblical king David by the artist Michelangelo, plus shirts, boxer shorts, hats, and a lot of other funny clothes to stick on it and dress it up. It was on their refrigerator right now. Everyone still took turns switching the clothes around.

Samantha looked farther to the left, over to the corner of the fortress, where a fountain bubbled. A giant stone man wearing a crown—and nothing else—stood on a pedestal in the center of a wide octagonal pool.

"The Fountain of Neptune," said Samantha.

Whenever Uncle Paul talked about Florence, he talked about Michelangelo's *David,* and he always mentioned the Fountain of Neptune, too.

Samantha looked down at the feet of Neptune, the god of the sea. Four enormous marble horses appeared to splash in the water.

"Sixteen horseshoes," said Samantha, nodding confidently.

She led Nipper to the edge of the fountain. Stone walls three feet high formed an octagon. At the corners were bronze statues of men, women, fish, and what she guessed were Roman gods. The statue in the center was enormous, even taller than Michelangelo's *David.* Neptune stood on a pedestal with circles on two sides, so it looked as if the horses were pulling him along in an underwater chariot.

Samantha took a closer look at the horses. From the edge of the pool, they seemed to be splashing and straining as they hauled Neptune through the water. Their mouths were open, as if gasping for air. Each horse pointed its face in a different direction.

She looked even closer, and noticed something odd. As she leaned forward over the fountain wall and stared at the bright marble faces, she saw a blue dot in one horse's nostril.

"There's something up with that horse," she told her brother, pointing. "Follow me into the fountain."

"I'm in," he said, and climbed up onto the wall ahead of her. Then he hopped into the water and waited.

Samantha wasn't as eager to go into the pool. She pulled herself up onto the stone wall and stopped to look back. She had been in this amazing historic city for less than an hour and had spent the entire time looking for a way to leave. Now the umbrella had led her to a mysterious dot in the middle of a horse's nose in the middle of a fountain.

In the many times she had thought about visiting the beautiful city of Florence, this was not what she'd had in mind. There were museums and cathedrals and historic palaces . . . and she was jumping into a fountain to find the quickest way home.

It wasn't fair.

She clutched the umbrella tightly as she hopped into the water and waded past Nipper toward the statues.

Water bubbled gently around them.

"Hey," said Nipper, gazing down at the floor of the pool. "There's money everywhere."

He knelt down and began to scoop up a handful of shiny coins. Samantha turned back and grabbed his arm.

"It's not yours," she said. "Those coins get collected for charity. And we're in the fountain to get out of here, remember?"

Nipper frowned for a minute. Then he nodded and stood back up, leaving the money where it was.

They splashed through the waist-deep water toward the center of the pool.

Samantha looked around. No one in the plaza had noticed them yet. She wasn't sure how long it would take before somebody did.

"Do you think this is where Uncle Paul's money came from?" Nipper asked, splashing behind her. "His letter mentioned underwater treasure. There are a lot of fountains around the world."

"I don't think so," said Samantha. "Didn't he say something about gold bars? Who throws gold bars into a fountain?"

Samantha abruptly stopped walking and Nipper ran into her. They'd come face to face with the four bright white marble stallions. She looked back at Nipper as she pointed to the face of the horse second from the right.

Nipper squinted at the horse for a moment. Then he stood up straight.

"Step aside," Nipper said loudly, pushing his sister out of the way. He raised a hand high in the air and wiggled his index finger.

"This is a nose-worthy situation," he declared, as if addressing an audience. "And I have been called upon to use my special talent!"

Samantha groaned. "Even in Florence, Italy, you are exceptionally gross."

Nipper plunged his finger deep inside the horse's dark nostril and pressed. Something gave, a little, and there was a click followed by four loud, low creaking noises. Somewhere deep below the street, it sounded like four giant toilets were flushing. Samantha and Nipper both looked down. The water directly beneath the horses' feet began to froth.

Nipper took one big step backward to where Samantha stood.

"My work here is done," he announced proudly, and folded his arms.

The water around the horses began to churn. It looked as if the marble herd was stampeding.

Samantha and Nipper inched back a bit more as the water started whipping more strongly and began to lap against the walls of the fountain.

"Ouch!" said Nipper as a wave tossed one of the

coins from the bottom of the fountain and smacked him hard on the cheek with it.

Both kids took another step back.

"Maybe we should get out of the pool for a minute," Nipper said nervously, rubbing his face where the coin had hit him.

But Samantha was staring at the horses' feet. A dark shape had appeared in the swirling water in front of them.

Nipper reached for his sister's hand, but she had already taken another big step back. Samantha turned and looked out from where they stood in the fountain. Several visitors around the plaza had begun to notice the watery spectacle.

"Mommy, it's a water show!" a boy wearing a New York Yankees T-shirt shouted, pointing at them.

"*Prego, non più pagliacci!*" wailed a woman standing next to him.

Samantha started to lose her footing. The fountain had become an angry squall.

"Wait!" she shouted to Nipper above the chaos. "I just remembered something Uncle Paul told us about *David*. That one's a copy. The real one is in the muse—"

The current yanked Samantha under the surface, ending her sentence in a gurgling "*Eeeee!*" She was being sucked toward the dark shape in front of the horses. She flailed her arms, slapping at the water helplessly, and slid into darkness.

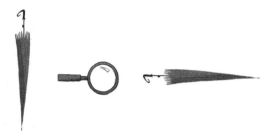

CHAPTER FOURTEEN

SLIP AND SLIDE

The magtrain ride to Paris had been smooth sailing. The pneumatic tube to Italy had been a bumpy tumble. Now, unexpectedly, Samantha faced a bruising, class 4 white-water challenge.

She dropped through the hole in the Fountain of Neptune, fell for about five feet, and landed with a splat on a narrow half-pipe track. Fountain water and coins rained down on her. A shallow but powerful current swept her forward.

Seconds later, she heard a splash and a thump as Nipper plopped down behind her. The current grew stronger and the rushing water propelled them along. The track became steeper and they rocketed down the slide.

They banked left and right, spiraling downward and bouncing off the walls of the U-shaped track.

Samantha clutched her umbrella close to her body and shut her eyes.

For a while she coasted along on her back. Then the current tossed and flipped her, and she was sliding headfirst. Water seemed to blast at her from all directions.

"Holy cow-a-bunga!" her brother shouted.

She opened her eyes just in time to see that the slide curved upward and ended with a ramp, spraying its contents into a giant funnel.

"Yow!" she shouted as she careened up and out of the half-pipe track and sailed through the air.

Samantha plunged into the funnel. Seconds later, she heard Nipper splash down behind her. She caught a glimpse of him every few seconds as they both swirled around and around in a vortex of water and foam. It dragged her to the center of the funnel. Then there was an incredibly loud *pop!* She shot through a tube at the bottom—and everything went white.

Samantha couldn't see anything but bubbles. She focused on her breathing as she rocketed along inside a bullet of foam. Slowly, the bubbles began to clear. She was back on a water slide. She coasted along again for what must have been minutes but seemed like hours.

Then the track made an extra-sharp turn and flung her out of the water. She bumped into a wall and tumbled down another dark slide.

Thump!

Samantha fell out onto a damp stone floor.

Thump!

Nipper spilled onto the floor beside her.

They both lay there quietly for a while, stunned, soggy, and sore.

Nipper sat up first. He shook his head from side to side. Then he did it five more times. It reminded Samantha of Dennis.

"That is the last time we go white-water rafting without a raft," she said.

She looked down and saw her fist clenched around the red umbrella. She'd been gripping it tightly the whole time. She eased up but didn't let go.

She rose to her feet carefully, using the umbrella to prop herself up.

The floor beneath them was a pattern of large tiles. Samantha recognized it immediately.

"France?" Nipper asked.

Samantha nodded. The water slide had dumped her and Nipper back into the room under the Louvre. A few yards away, they could see a blinking red dot.

"Magtrain. Home," she said.

They walked carefully toward the faint light, their shoes squishing on the floor with every step. The glowing dot was the oval button near the center seat of the magtrain car.

They climbed aboard the familiar car and took their places. Samantha tapped the button and the tiny hairs on her arms stood up. The rails began to glow, and she and Nipper sped away through the tunnel.

Samantha pushed some soggy hair away from her face and leaned back in the seat. Her neck and her arms were sore from the water ride. If giant pneumatic tubes weren't a smart way to travel, then international water-slides were completely stupid.

Then she looked over at the umbrella resting against the rail. It was full of secrets . . . and danger . . . and pointless pain and aggravation.

Did Uncle Paul really think he was giving her a present? So far, it had gotten her bounced around, soaked, bruised, and almost sliced by ninjas. Maybe the smelly ninjas were planning to kill whoever had the umbrella, and that's why he'd passed it to her and run away.

"Thanks a lot, Pajama Paul," she said softly.

Samantha figured they had about twenty minutes before they would be back in Seattle. She took out her notebook and inspected it. It was damp on the outside, but the pages inside were still dry. She began to write:

If someone puts you in grave danger and then you have to leave the beautiful city of Florence in a hurry, look for Neptune's Fountain.

Wade into the water, up to the statue with four horses. Face the second horse from the right and stick your finger in his nose. . . .

RMS *Titanic*

The RMS *Titanic* was a British passenger ship that sank in the North Atlantic Ocean during its maiden voyage.

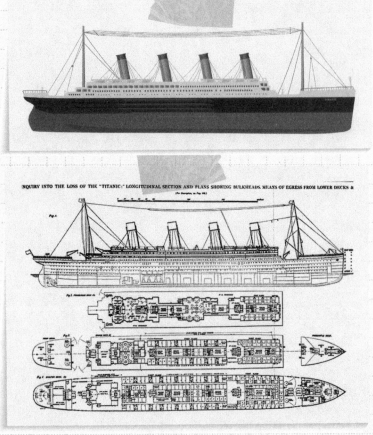

It was the largest and most luxurious vessel of its day, and its passengers included some of the richest people in the history of the world.

It had a state-of-the-art design with a series of innovative watertight compartments that were supposed to make the ship "unsinkable."

Tragically, the *Titanic* collided with an iceberg in the early morning of April 15, 1912. It filled with water, snapped in two, and sank.

There were not enough lifeboats aboard to carry the passengers, and more than fifteen hundred people were lost at sea.

Some people question why the *Titanic* sank so quickly.

* * *

If you have scuba equipment, you can reach the back half of the *Titanic* from a tunnel that runs below the North Atlantic Ocean. This section of the sunken vessel includes the engine room, coal storage, and several of the ship's secret treasure vaults.

Most of the gold bars and other valuable items that these secret vaults held have been removed from the wreck. An estimated $2,400,000,000 has vanished from the ship—an amount of precious metal that would have far exceeded the ship's weight capacity.

If you take a closer look at things, however, it is still possible to come across treasure when you explore the ruins along the cold, dark ocean floor.

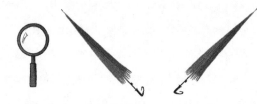

CHAPTER FIFTEEN

WATCH OUT FOR THE RAIN

As soon as Samantha and Nipper made it home, they changed into clean, dry clothes and went to the kitchen. Neither of them had eaten anything all day, other than when Nipper munched on a few bread cubes.

They made themselves sandwiches and were just cleaning up when their parents came in through the side door.

"Sorry we're so late, kids," said Mrs. Spinner. "I hope you weren't worried about us."

Mr. Spinner leaned his umbrella against the wall and started to hang up his coat but stopped. He studied his children for a moment. It was the right number of kids, but they were wearing different clothes than they'd been wearing that morning. Samantha's hair was a mess, and she looked like she'd been blasted in the face by a garden hose. Nipper had a bruise about the size of a quarter on his cheek.

"You're looking a little rough around the edges, you two," observed their father. "Did something happen while we were gone?"

Samantha and her brother glanced at each other.

"How was the Pet Expo?" Samantha asked, changing the subject.

"Ahh . . . what a fine show," Mr. Spinner declared, not even noticing that she hadn't answered his question. He turned and finished hanging up his coat.

Then he bent down and grabbed their pug with both hands.

"Look what we got," he said, holding Dennis up in front of them.

"We already had that dog," said Nipper.

"Very funny," their dad said, twisting the pug around to show off a new pet accessory. A wide plastic ring curved around Dennis's neck just above his sparkling collar with the giant blue gem.

A very faint buzzing sound came from the dog.

"It's a Blinky Barker light," their dad said, dropping Dennis back onto the floor. "Show 'em what you can do, old pal."

"Wruf!" the little dog yapped, and a lightbulb turned on inside the new collar. It reflected off the jewels on his gold collar and the facets of the big walnut-sized diamond, lighting up the room in a dazzling display of light.

Mr. Spinner smiled. "What a splendid use of science," he said, watching Dennis trot off to the living room.

Mrs. Spinner walked over and joined the conversation. "It was a strange day at the expo," she said.

"Oh, yes," their father chimed in. "We had an encounter with a strange group of people, all dressed in black."

Samantha and Nipper glanced at each other again.

"We saw them following Dennis around the convention hall," said Mrs. Spinner. "Then they started following your father and me."

"They seemed to think they were being sneaky," Mr. Spinner added. "But we noticed right away because they smelled terrible. Like smoldering lamp cords, or sulfurous filament epoxy."

"Here's the strange part," their mother continued. "While one of them tried to get my attention, the other one grabbed our umbrella. He opened it up in the middle of the convention hall. He got really angry and threw it on the floor."

"They walked away without saying anything," said their father.

Mrs. Spinner went to the kitchen counter and began sorting through the day's mail.

"What is it with everyone and their umbrellas?" she wondered as she opened an envelope.

"Well, dear, this *is* Seattle," Mr. Spinner reminded her.

Samantha decided not to say anything about smelly ninjas or umbrella snatchers just then. She shot her brother a quick look to keep him quiet.

Mrs. Spinner unfolded five pages of blue paper. It was a new Unexplained Vanishing Person Form.

"Didn't we already fill out three of those?" asked Mr. Spinner.

A week after Uncle Paul went missing, two notices arrived. One was a death certificate for "Flipflop P. Wafflemaker." Another was an official warning to be on the lookout for an eight-year-old girl in a yellow polka-dot blouse who had gone missing in 1973.

Many more incorrect forms and crazy, mixed-up files had come since then.

This one requested additional information for "Pablo Rotación."

"I think the police officers who came to our house were clowns," Mrs. Spinner sighed.

While their parents worked together at the table

filling out the new form, Samantha and Nipper left the house through the kitchen door.

"Flipflop P. Wafflemaker." Nipper chuckled as they headed across the driveway.

"Pablo Rotación." Samantha giggled, then stopped when she realized what she'd said. "Wait. I think that's Spanish for Paul Spinner."

"I don't think anyone's ever going to get Uncle Paul's name right," said Nipper.

Samantha became more serious. "And I don't think Uncle Paul is dead, either," she said.

They stopped at the foot of the stairs to Uncle Paul's apartment over the garage.

"You keep saying that," Nipper told her. "But we've been halfway around the world and haven't seen or heard anything about Uncle Paul at all."

He looked up at the stairs.

"And now we're right back where we started."

Samantha pulled the throwing star from her pocket and waved it at Nipper.

"No," she said. "Ninjas are hunting for umbrellas on two continents. And this is a clue."

Samantha and Nipper climbed the stairs next to the garage, entered their uncle's one-room apartment, and began to investigate everything from scratch. They studied all the walls and windowsills. They crawled along the floor and searched under the sofa. They were both sure that, somewhere, there was a clue about ninjas who smell or uncles who just go missing.

"What exactly are we looking for?" Nipper asked.

"I have no idea," said Samantha. "Another throwing star . . . or a note that says 'I'm sorry you won't get to spend any time in Florence.' Maybe there's a book about umbrellas."

They stood back up and began to explore the bookshelves. Samantha started with the books on the top shelf and Nipper started from the bottom. There were too many to read. Systematically, they inspected the spine of each book. Some had titles printed in English. Others had words in completely unidentifiable languages, if they were words at all. Other books just had symbols on them.

Halfway across the bottom shelf, Nipper gasped. He gestured for Samantha to come look at a thick book bound in red leather.

Three engraved symbols ran down the spine: an arrow, a slingshot, and a ninja throwing star. Nipper yanked the book from the shelf and stood up.

" 'Encyclopedia Missilium,' " he read dramatically. He flipped through the pages and stopped about a third of the way through the book.

" 'Chapter Four,' " he read. " 'Shuriken and Those Who Throw Them.' "

Samantha held up the throwing star so they could

both see the image engraved in the center. Then she turned the star over. An ornate crown with angled swords decorated each side. Nipper flipped forward a few more pages. Then he held the book up for both of them to read.

The Royal Academy of International Ninjas (aka the RAIN)

The RAIN is an international crime syndicate. The organization is designed to consist of two dozen members at all times. Said members include twenty-three martial arts masters and a trained monkey. They specialize in stealth, murder, and theft.

They have stolen a super-secret diagram giving them access to hidden doorways and transportation networks around the globe. This has transformed them from a mediocre outlaw gang to a worldwide criminal menace.

The RAIN gathers twice a month to plan crimes. Each meeting's leader is set on a rotating calendar and is responsible for chairing the meeting and for bringing snacks. Together, the ninjas of the RAIN have perpetrated some of the most daring art robberies and bank heists in history.

They remain at large to this day.

"That's it!" Samantha exclaimed. She marched around the room shouting at her brother with excitement. "Uncle Paul told me to watch out for the *RAIN!*"

Nipper stood still in front of the bookcase. He quickly did some math in his head. Twenty-three martial arts masters plus one. Twenty-four meetings.

"Once a year, there's a meeting that nobody wants to go to," he said.

"What are you taking about?" asked Samantha.

"Nobody wants snacks from a monkey," he pointed out.

The Sewers of Paris

Paris has a sewer system different from that of any other city in the world.

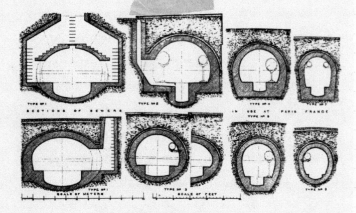

ITINÉRAIRES DES PREMIÈRES LIGNES D'OMNIBUS EN 1828.
Dressé d'après les documents par A. Meunier. — (Collection Charles Simond.)

The first sewer tunnels were built in Paris in 1370, and the government has been adding to them ever since.

Today, there are more than a thousand miles of tunnels bringing freshwater into the city and taking sewage out.

Many of the tunnels are also lined with delivery tubes. Up until a few years ago, these formed an air-powered mail system responsible for sending plastic cylinders throughout the city. Letters and small packages were delivered from building to building through the pneumatic tubes.

* * *

Recently, the Royal Academy of International Ninjas lost their top-secret blueprint of hidden passages around the world. They have been stuck in Paris ever since and they use the sewer system as their headquarters. From there they prey upon the citizens and treasures of Paris.

Squeezing through drains, exhaust pipes, and garbage chutes has infused them with the stench and sewage of the City of Light. It has turned them into stink-bandits, known to the French authorities as Les Bandits Putrides.

This has made it difficult for the ninjas to travel. If they venture beyond the sewers for any length of time, their strong odor gives them away.

The RAIN is very, very unhappy about being stuck in Paris. They want the Super-Secret Plans back—now!

CHAPTER SIXTEEN

NET WORK

Samantha and Nipper stood in the center of their uncle's apartment for a while. They felt triumphant.

"Uncle Paul was warning me about the ninjas all along," said Samantha.

"That's great," said Nipper. "Now what's our next move?"

Samantha stood there, tapping one finger on her chin as she tried to come up with an answer. She looked excited for a moment. Then she looked serious again. Then she looked thoughtful. She had nothing.

"We've just got to keep looking," said Samantha. "Somehow, we're missing an important clue that can lead us to Uncle Paul."

She started to pace around the room impatiently.

"Why are those ninjas so smelly?" she asked, talking faster and louder. "And how did they find Dennis and Mom and Dad at the Pet Expo?"

She looked at the coffee table. Then she walked over and grabbed the hula hoop trophy. She waved it at the note pinned to the wall.

"And what's so special about waffles?" she shouted dramatically.

"We don't even know that Uncle Paul's alive, Sam!" Nipper shouted back at her. "And I don't want to puzzle over this place anymore!" He rubbed the bruise on his cheek and cried, "I got hit in the face with money today and I didn't even get to keep it!"

He gestured toward the window. The sun was starting to set.

"It's getting dark," he continued, even louder. "I'm tired, and I—" Nipper stopped mid-complaint and stared.

The sun was sinking lower in the sky, and a nearby streetlamp switched on, shining directly through the windows of the apartment. It cast a web of dark lines from the shadow of the basketball net onto the wall across the room.

Samantha turned and saw what her brother was staring at.

Lines crisscrossed the wall, one running diagonally over Uncle Paul's note.

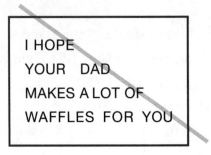

I HOPE
YOUR   DAD
MAKES A LOT OF
WAFFLES FOR YOU

The line crossed through four letters: *E-D-F-U*.

"Edfu?" Nipper asked.

Samantha was already reaching for a large atlas on the shelf next to the *Encyclopedia Missilium*. She opened the book, turned to the index, and scanned the list of cities and countries.

"Edfu, Egypt," she answered, and closed the book.

CHAPTER SEVENTEEN

OPERATION FLIP-FLOP

Samantha remembered Edfu from their first visit to the magtrain station. The name was one of those carved into the arches above the tunnels. At the time, she'd had no idea what "Edfu" meant or if it was even a real word.

Now it was their best, clearest clue to what happened to their missing uncle.

"Tomorrow's a big day," she told Nipper as they marched back across the driveway. She held the umbrella tightly by the middle, pointing it toward the house.

"This time we're going to be prepared and we're going to do things right."

It occurred to her that she sounded a little bit like a general or a football coach. That was just fine with her.

"We'll bring snacks," she said.

"Check," Nipper answered.

"We're going to bring some emergency money," she said.

"Check," said Nipper.

"Umbrella."

"Check."

"Magnifying glass."

"Hand lens," Nipper corrected her. "And check."

Samantha opened the side door of their house, stepped inside, flipped on the kitchen light, and continued.

"And we'll need some light," she said. "I'm tired of stumbling around in the dark."

"Yes," said Nipper. "And we're bringing Dennis."

Samantha looked her brother in the eye and thought about this for a few seconds.

"Okay," she said.

"Meet here first thing in the morning?" Nipper asked.

She looked over at the refrigerator. A note in her mother's handwriting was held to the door by a magnet shaped like a pair of boxer shorts.

CHINCHILLA FESTIVAL
SUNDAY
10 A.M.

"Let's wait until Mom and Dad leave," she said. "Ten-fifteen."

Nipper gave her two thumbs up.

Samantha started to march up the stairs. Then she caught herself and stopped. She peered up to make sure her parents weren't in the hall. Then she tiptoed quietly to her bedroom and went right to sleep.

At 10:15 a.m., Samantha went down to the kitchen.

Nipper was already waiting for her with Dennis panting happily at his feet.

"I've got snacks," he said, holding up a plastic bag filled with crackers.

Dennis watched the bag carefully.

"I researched Egyptian money," said Samantha. "There's no way we're going to get Egyptian pounds quickly."

"Don't worry," said Nipper. "I've got us covered. One hundred."

He held up a crisp bill and waved it in the air.

"Wait," said Samantha. "Let me take a closer look at that bill."

"Uncle Paul gave me this hundred for my birthday last year," he said, and slipped it into his front pocket.

Dennis kept watch on the bag of crackers.

Samantha felt her pocket to make sure she had the little black journal.

"Wait here and I'll find some light," she said.

She headed out of the kitchen, through the living room, and into Mr. Spinner's study at the back of the house. There were stacks of cardboard boxes everywhere, bulging with papers, electrical cables, and strange tools. There was a framed portrait of George Washington Carver on one wall. Between a tower of rubber bins and a trash can filled with rolled-up posters, she found his little wooden desk.

Samantha knew that her dad kept samples of experimental lightbulbs in the desk drawer. She fished around until she found a small padded envelope labeled "X-27B." Sure enough, there was a tiny bulb inside.

"This won't be missed," she said, holding it up between two fingers and examining it. Then she hurried back to the kitchen.

"Dog, please," she said.

Her brother hoisted Dennis from the floor and held him out to her. The dog collar buzzed softly. She removed the bulb from the Blinky Barker and replaced it with the X-27B.

"Show 'em what you can do, old pal," Nipper, imitating Mr. Spinner's voice, called to Dennis.

"Wruf!" the pug barked on cue.

Instantly, bright white light bathed the room.

Powerful beams shot from the collar, reflecting off windows, framed photos, a silver travel mug, and a dozen other surfaces in the kitchen. Some of the rays illuminated the gems on Dennis's collar, adding a swirling, scintillating light show to the room.

"Yow!" said Samantha, shielding her face with both hands.

"Argh," said Nipper, dropping the dog and turning away with his eyes shut tight. "So . . . very . . . bright."

"Bark, old pal!" Samantha said, not even trying to sound like their dad.

Dennis gave her a quick "Wruf!"

The collar turned off.

It took a full minute for them to recover from the blinding glare.

"That," said Nipper, rubbing his eyes, "is one heck of a lightbulb!"

Samantha looked him straight in the eye and pointed at him.

"Don't forget to remind me to put it back when we get home."

"Absolutely. I won't," said Nipper.

They took two pairs of sunglasses from the junk bowl on the counter.

Samantha left a note on the refrigerator for their parents saying that they were going to an all-day party at the Bogden-Loople house next door. It was going to be a triple-feature movie party and they wouldn't be home until after dinner.

"Why are you lying to Mom and Dad about going to the Bogden-Looples'?" asked Nipper.

"I hate to do it," she said. "But Uncle Paul is in danger, and he needs us to find him."

Then she added, "What would happen if Mom decided to call Morgan Bogan and ask about us?" She grinned a little and waited for Nipper to think.

Nipper grinned, too. Everything their neighbor said was preposterous. Of course he'd confirm that they were at his house.

"You are brilliant, big sister." He bowed to her. "But more important, you are *sneaky!*"

Dennis found a cracker that had missed the bag. It was stuck to one leg of the kitchen table a few inches from the floor. Then they all left the house.

With the umbrella, the hand lens, sunglasses, crackers, money, and a pug wearing an extremely powerful light-bulb, Samantha and Nipper headed down the block to an ordinary-looking mailbox.

In minutes, they were standing at the corner of Prospect Street and Thirteenth Avenue. The Volunteer

Park water tower rose a block away as they faced the mailbox. This time, they didn't need to check the Super-Secret Plans.

"Three times," Nipper reminded his sister.

Samantha reached for the mailbox handle.

Suddenly Dennis sniffed the air and growled.

"Sam—" Nipper reached out and stopped her. "Do you smell burned bacon, dirty socks, and sardines?"

Clang! A throwing star sailed between them and caromed off the top of the mailbox.

CHAPTER EIGHTEEN

DOWNHILL FAST

"Stop!" someone shouted. "Don't move!"

Samantha and Nipper couldn't help it. They turned around.

A squad of shrouded bandits stood in a long, smelly line. One of them held up three shuriken with his left hand.

"Well, okay," he said, sounding irritated. "You can turn around, but don't move again."

Before Samantha or Nipper could do or say anything, the ninjas sprang forward and formed a circle around them. They were surrounded.

Samantha quickly counted the ninjas. There were twenty of them. They were all dressed in black, and every one was soiled from head to toe. One of the ninjas was much shorter than the others. The stink was unbearable.

"Hand over the umbrella now," said the ninja with the throwing stars. "Or we'll have to cut this meeting short."

With his free hand he drew his sword. One after the other, the ninjas unsheathed menacing silver blades. A wave of reflected light rippled around the circle.

Samantha had seen what a single samurai sword could do to a loaf of French bread. Now she faced twenty of them. She looked around the circle again. She and her brother were trapped.

She had no idea what to do. Slowly, she pulled the umbrella from her shoulder.

"Sam?" Nipper asked.

Samantha's heart ached. She wasn't just handing over the umbrella. She was giving away her only chance to find Uncle Paul.

Sadly, she held out the Super-Secret Plans.

"Smart girl," the ninja snarled, stepping forward. He tucked his sword away. Then he reached out a grimy hand and grabbed the closed umbrella.

"We spent six weeks hidden on a garbage barge to get here," he said, waving the umbrella at them. "It was the only way we could travel here without being smelled. Do you know what monkeys do in the middle of the ocean when—"

The ninja's words were cut off in a blur of fur as Dennis leaped forward with stunning speed and precision.

Maybe he saw a moment for greatness. Maybe he wanted to save his friends. Or maybe it was because the ninja had just smeared the umbrella with bacon grease and sardine juice.

Dennis seized the umbrella and bit down. Then he was off. He bolted into Volunteer Park.

"*Breeep!*" the shortest ninja howled. He dropped his sword and banged his knuckles against the ground several times. Then he grabbed the sword and stood up straight again.

Samantha and Nipper pushed their way through the confused ninjas and took off after their hero pug.

It was a five-block run down the length of Volunteer Park, past the art museum and the water tower, around the reservoir and in between some Frisbee players enjoying precious hours in the sun.

Samantha and Nipper caught up with Dennis just as he reached the busy street at the bottom of the park. He stopped at the corner and looked up at them.

"Good boy," said Nipper. He took out the plastic bag, opened it, and tossed a cracker to the dog.

Dennis dropped the umbrella and caught the cracker in midair.

Nipper picked up the umbrella and handed it back to Samantha.

"That makes four ninjas in Paris and twenty in Seattle," said Nipper.

"How did they find us here?" Samantha asked.

"I don't know," he answered. "*We're* not the ones you can smell from a mile away."

Samantha nodded. "They must have some special way of tracking us," she said. They turned left and sped into Capitol Hill's business district, threading their way through shoppers, joggers, bicycles, and baby strollers.

"Excuse me," said Samantha as she bumped into a woman juggling for people in line at a coffee cart.

"Sorry!" said Nipper as he slipped between two men doing yoga outside a café.

As they dodged parking meters and dog walkers, the smell of kerosene and used kitty litter began to catch up with them. The sound of split-toe ninja slippers slapping pavement began to grow louder.

"They're going to chop us into little cubes!" Nipper cried, gasping for air. "We'll be just like that French bread!"

Samantha looked around quickly. They were in the middle of the block between Coffee Mania and Seattle

Fabric Center. They couldn't outrun the ninjas. And there were too many of them to fight.

"Hold my hand," she told Nipper.

"What?" he asked his sister. "I like you, too, Sam, but right now we—"

Samantha grabbed his hand, yanked hard, and pulled him into Seattle Fabric Center.

Some people love craft projects that involve sewing, knitting, or needlepoint. Other people become drowsy the moment they hear someone say "yarn" or "crochet." Samantha Spinner was somewhere between the two camps. But she was confident that her brother and the twenty ninjas chasing them fell solidly into the second group.

Samantha led Nipper through the front door of the store. They passed a young woman sitting behind a glass case of ribbons and zipper parts. It looked like she was knitting a skull and crossbones, but they had no time to ask her about it. They turned and sped down an aisle lined on both sides with rotating racks of colorful felt. Then they dove behind a bin labeled "Misprinted Flannel 90% Off!" and crouched out of sight.

Immediately Nipper started yawning.

"No daw-awgs!" the woman called out in a singsong voice.

Dennis scampered around the corner and squeezed between Samantha and Nipper.

"This is the most boring store I've ever seen," said Nipper. He looked around at the displays of thread and bobbins. A long sheet of woven fabric with gold braid trim dangled from the ceiling.

"Why on earth would anyone want to—"

"Shhhh!" Samantha glared at her brother.

The store was nearly silent. They could hear the muffled clicking of the woman's needles as she knit, and the faint buzz from Dennis's collar.

Nipper's eyelids were half closed and his breathing was becoming slower and deeper as he petted a stack of folded lace tablecloths.

They heard the door swing open and the sound of forty sticky feet creeping one by one onto linoleum.

"Nipper?" Samantha whispered.

Her brother was sound asleep.

Samantha began to get drowsy, too. Then the strong smell of rotten pickles, corroded batteries, and moldy cat food hit her, and she snapped out of it. She could hear the ninjas shuffling around the store. They were opening and closing display cases and poking at spools of fabric and bunting with their samurai swords.

Peeking through a gap between bins, she saw two legs in black tights approaching. Someone was getting close to their aisle. She held Dennis by his muzzle to keep him from growling.

When she turned to peek through the gap again, the legs were still there, but they were wobbling.

Then the ninja fell to the floor like a bag of wet sand. He was fast asleep.

Seconds later, she heard what sounded like nineteen more bags of wet sand hitting the floor. Ninja by ninja, the RAIN had collapsed onto the floor of Seattle Fabric Center. Samantha waited, holding her nose against the stench. Soon the sound of twenty snoring ninjas filled the store.

Samantha stood up and hoisted her sleeping brother over one shoulder. She climbed out from behind the bin and, as quietly as she could, carried him to the front of the store.

"Happens all the time," said the woman. She paused and sniffed the air disapprovingly several times but didn't look up from her knitting.

Samantha pushed open the door and held it for Dennis, then followed him out, carefully balancing her unconscious cargo.

She carried Nipper for half a block, set him on his feet, and shook him a few times.

"Wake up," she said. She held out the umbrella and used it to point toward the park in the distance. "Egypt is that way."

CHAPTER NINETEEN

PRINTS OF EGYPT

Once again, Samantha and Nipper stood in front of the mailbox with their pug at their feet.

Samantha carefully opened and closed the metal flap three times and the steel chamber rose from the ground on cue. As soon as it locked into place, Sam, Nipper, and Dennis stepped inside and headed down the secret staircase.

They paused in the center of the dark room. Sam and Nipper both put on their sunglasses.

"Show 'em what you can do, old pal," said Samantha. This time, she did a fairly good impression of her father.

"Wruf!" said Dennis.

The X-27B switched on, bathing the room in bright white light.

For the first time, they got a true look at the mag-train station.

The floor was a colorful mosaic of tiles that formed a map of the world. A different type of stone had been used for each country. Germany was slate. Brazil was turquoise. India was rose quartz. There were hundreds of colors and textures.

Art deco columns stood between the portals to the magtrain tunnels. Stained-glass rings covered each pillar from top to bottom, reflecting the light up to the ceiling.

Just a few feet above the kids' heads, the chamber ceiling extended into a shallow dome that looked like it was made of white marble. Hundreds of shiny golden objects dangled from the dome, glittering as they slowly turned. They were small sculptures: a bird, a flower, a fruit, a statue, a famous landmark.

Samantha and her brother stood and stared. They looked up, down, and all around, taking everything in.

"There is so much to do," Samantha said softly.

She reached up and touched a golden model of the Lincoln Memorial. Through the columns, she could see Abraham Lincoln.

"There are so many places to go," she added.

"Look!" Nipper shouted, snapping Samantha out of her thoughts. He was pointing at the archways surrounding them. "We can see all the writing now."

With the room lit so brightly, smaller words were visible beneath the large carved letters.

DYNAMITE
Have a blast in the Pacific Northwest

PARIS
City of Light

BARABOO
Town of clowns

DUCK
North Carolina is coming at you

ZZYZX
California's spelling-bee favorite

EDFU
Phun for pharaohs

WAGGA WAGGA
Planes, trains, and kangaroos

WAHOO
Nebraska loves you

EXIT
To the Emerald City

Samantha pointed up at the word *Edfu* with the umbrella and waved the metal tip under the small writing.

"Okay," she said. "Let's have some *phun*."

They both took one more moment to marvel at the magnificent chamber around them and then marched into the tunnel labeled "Edfu."

They took their familiar places in the magtrain car and Dennis hopped onto Samantha's lap. Thirty-three minutes later, they stood in a new station, studying the Plans by the light of the X-27B.

After exiting the magtrain, Samantha, Nipper, and Dennis had followed a ramp from the train tracks up into a small square room. A ladder that led up to a hole in the ceiling was attached to one wall. An enormous falcon was painted on another wall. It stood at attention and wore a tall cylindrical hat.

"I recognize that bird. It's the Egyptian god Honus," said Nipper. "Uncle Paul told us about him."

"You're close," said Samantha. "That's the god Horus."

"Are you sure?" he asked. "I'm pretty sure I remember the name Honus."

"He was on your baseball card. Don't you remember?" Samantha asked.

Nipper didn't answer, though, because he was already climbing the ladder. Samantha popped open the umbrella quickly.

"Wait," she called. "I'll find us a secret hidden exit."

Nipper stopped climbing. "Uh, ladder?" he said,

pointing to the opening directly above him. "Come on," he said, and kept going. He pushed open a round hatch above him, and light spilled down from the world outside.

"Close the umbrella and bring the dog," he added, and disappeared through the hole.

Samantha shrugged. "That works, too," she said.

She stood there for a moment, thinking about all the things, secret or obvious, that weren't on the umbrella. She closed the Plans and slung them over her shoulder, tucked Dennis under one arm, and started climbing. It was a tricky maneuver, scaling the ladder with a pug under her arm, so she climbed carefully. Finally, she got to the hole in the ceiling and stopped. Nipper stood outside, waiting. She passed Dennis up to her brother and quickly joined him.

They were standing on the head of an enormous stone bird statue exactly like the one in the picture. They were just tall enough that their own heads poked out of the bird's hat.

"Crow's nest," said Nipper.

Falcon's nest, Samantha thought, but she didn't bother to say it out loud.

Dennis barked and switched off the light in his collar.

They were perched above a sun-drenched courtyard surrounded by ancient ruins. They faced a massive stone structure. It was almost a hundred feet high, with walls that sloped so that the whole building looked like a giant upside-down *W*. It was covered with carvings of Egyptian men and women and animal-headed gods.

A shorter building, about half as high, stood behind them. It had round columns that fanned out at the top like stone palm trees. A steady stream of visitors came and went through a metal gate behind the columns.

"Let's go there," said Samantha, pointing to the gate.

They waited until there was no one in sight. Then they climbed out of the hat and slid down the back of the falcon's neck, over its body, and down its stone tail feathers.

"Are you sure that's where we need to go?" asked Nipper, following closely behind Samantha and Dennis.

"I'm not," she said.

"Are you even sure we're supposed to be here in Edfu?" he asked. "Maybe those letters on the wall were just a coincidence."

Samantha recognized that sound. It was the sound of her brother getting impatient. She adjusted the umbrella over her shoulder as she walked faster, passing between the columns and through the gate.

Glass walls enclosed a lobby to the museum beyond. Several signs on metal bases lined the way to a wide pair of glass doors. Each sign welcomed visitors in a different language. Samantha recognized Arabic, English, French, Spanish, and several others.

She pointed to the English-language sign.

OUR NEW EXHIBIT

DISCOVERIES FROM THE PTOLEMAIC DYNASTY

DON'T MISS OPENING DAY!

"I don't think that's a coincidence," she said.

Nipper nodded in agreement.

They removed their sunglasses and pushed one of the doors open. Dennis padded happily behind.

As soon as they entered the lobby, a woman in a uniform stepped in front of them. She held up one hand and pointed to the dog with the other.

Samantha picked up Dennis and cradled him like a baby. Then she looked up at the guard with a hopeful smile.

"*Min fadlik?*" Samantha asked in perfect Arabic.

The guard look surprised, then nodded, with a wide approving grin.

"You said 'please' so nicely, young American lady," she said. "I do not see a small dog with a sparkling collar." She waved them in.

"See?" Samantha told Nipper quietly. "If you're nice, it opens doors for you."

"Sure," Nipper replied, even quieter. "But it doesn't get your Yankees back."

They entered the large room. Hundreds of ancient artifacts were on display around them. A sacred boat appeared next to a chair on long poles that servants had used to carry Egyptian nobles from place to place. Fragments of statues rested on pedestals in a dozen locations.

At the center of the exhibit, a long sheet of woven fabric with gold braid trim dangled inside a glass case. The fabric was painted in black, green, and bright orange.

A museum guide beckoned. "Come closer," he said. "This is our most recent find, and we are very excited about it."

The Spinners approached the man as he gestured toward the exhibit.

"This fantastically preserved artifact was discovered pinned to a wall inside the Temple of Horus," he told them. "Nobody knows how it got there."

He paused and looked at each of them for dramatic effect.

"Archaeologists are still trying to determine the age of this fantastic object," he continued. "It may be only a few years old, or it may be several thousands of years old."

He pointed to a small round detail in the bottom

corner and lowered his voice to a soft whisper. "Our only clue is down here. This mysterious symbol looks a lot like English letters," he said. "Don't you agree?"

"What was that last part?" asked Nipper, beginning to feel very nervous.

Samantha leaned in to examine the tiny mark. It was a big letter *S* surrounding the letters *F* and *C*.

"Up here," the guide announced enthusiastically, "these four illustrations tell the story called 'The Traveler and the Monkey King.'"

Colorful drawings featured animals, gods, and several familiar-looking Egyptian symbols. The central figures in all four pictures were a human-sized monkey wearing a black robe and a man in a gold vest. Only, instead of the white skirt of ancient Egyptian dress, the man wore green plaid pants that looked a lot like pajamas.

And his shoes were, unmistakably, orange flip-flops.

Samantha smiled.

It was Uncle Paul.

CHAPTER TWENTY

THE TRAVELER AND THE MONKEY KING

"In ancient times, a monkey king danced round and round in the golden warmth of the sun," said the museum guide, interpreting the object in the display case.

He swept his hand up to point at the first illustration. It showed the monkey waving both its arms in the air. A dark circle looped around its waist.

"It looks to me like that monkey's using a hula hoop," said Nipper.

"While the king danced and danced, a traveler came and stole his magic spear," continued the guide, waving his hand below the second illustration.

In that picture, the man in orange shoes tiptoed behind the monkey. He held a red triangle with a J-shaped handle at the bottom.

"That spear looks like an umbrella," said Nipper.

Samantha glanced at her own umbrella, then back at the exhibit.

"The traveler gave the magic spear to a young woman who was very brave and very clever," the guide explained.

The third picture showed the man running away from a pack of identical warriors dressed all in black. He was handing the red triangle to a young woman.

Samantha smiled.

"The traveler knew that everyone he loved was in terrible danger. So he ran to a land far, far away," the guide concluded.

In the final picture, the man stood beside a tower. It looked like the Washington Monument, but it was covered in Egyptian symbols.

The guide bowed his head to show that he was finished.

"What kind of stupid story is that?" Nipper asked loudly. "What could it possibly mean?"

The museum guide held out his hands, palms up.

"I haven't the foggiest idea," he said, and shrugged.

Samantha tugged at Nipper's sleeve and pulled him a few feet off to the side.

"That artifact is definitely not thousands of years old," she told her brother.

Samantha put Dennis on the floor. Then she took out her journal and drew some letters at the top of a blank page.

She began to sketch the tower from the fourth illustration of the story.

The Temple of Horus

The Temple of Horus is located in the city of Edfu near the banks of the river Nile. It is one of the best-preserved temples in Egypt.

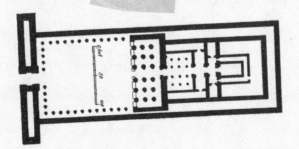

Completed in 57 BC, it is a shrine to the falcon-headed god, Horus. Carvings on the wall reveal many details about the culture of Egypt thousands of years ago.

In ancient times, the temple was the center of sacred festivals. Today, it is a major tourist attraction. Millions of people visit Edfu every year.

* * *

Look for a sacred boat resting on a pedestal. There is a secret passageway below it. If you press on one of the panels of the pedestal, it will swing inward to reveal a ramp. This leads to a hidden tomb directly below the Temple of Horus.

These secret chambers were built five thousand years before the Temple of Horus. The Ptolemaic Egyptians didn't even know about this tomb.

There is no natural light inside. You will have to bring your own lamp. The hallways, rooms, and everything in them have remained undisturbed since they were built—until very recently.

CHAPTER TWENTY-ONE

LOOT, LOOT, LOOT FOR THE HOME TEAM

Normally, Nipper was the not the first person that Samantha would want anywhere near her while she tried to sketch an artifact. Yet there they were. She kneeled on the ground as she copied the picture of the tower slowly and carefully. Nipper stood and waited . . . and fidgeted.

While his sister was still drawing in her journal, he picked up the umbrella and popped it open.

"Let's see," he said as he scanned the lining through his magnifying glass.

He lowered the umbrella and looked around. Then he snapped the umbrella shut and dropped it back on the floor next to Samantha.

"Sam," he said excitedly. "There's a secret door just across the way. I think it's underneath a boat."

"Let me finish," said Samantha, drawing faster. "I'm almost done."

Nipper walked away from the exhibit.

Dennis trotted after him.

Samantha copied the last few symbols. Then she looked up.

Nipper was gone.

Quickly, she got to her feet and slung the umbrella over her shoulder. Looking left and right, she marched through several pairs of stone columns until she reached a model of a ceremonial riverboat.

The boat stood balanced on a wide rectangular pedestal. Samantha saw a small panel on one side of the base. The panel had been pushed open.

"Nipper," she muttered to herself.

It had to be the secret door her brother had been yammering about while she was trying to sketch. She walked up to it and crouched to look inside. She could make out a long, low passageway that sloped downward and was punctuated by a very bright light in the distance.

". . . and Dennis," she added.

Samantha put on her sunglasses, got down on her hands and knees, and crawled through the opening. She stopped and twisted around to push the panel shut; then she headed toward the light.

She crawled for about thirty feet until the tunnel let out into a wide, round room.

She stood up and dusted off her pants.

Dennis sat across from her on the far side of the room, happily munching from the bag of crackers. The Blinky Barker bathed everything in bright white light. It reflected off silver panels that hung on the walls of the chamber and out through exits to the left and right. With each chew, blue sparkles swirled around the room as the light reflected off the big blue gem on his collar. The illumination revealed colorful drawings and symbols covering the ceiling and every inch of the wall.

There were large, dark gaps to the left and right where open doorways led to spaces beyond.

Samantha started to step forward—and stopped. A black circle took up most of the floor of the room. It was a deep, dark pit, surrounded by a narrow ledge.

She heard several faint grunting sounds. Fearfully, she inched forward and gazed into the hole.

"Nipper? Are you down there?" she asked.

She peered into the pit and saw smooth walls that extended far beyond the light from Dennis's collar. It had to be at least fifty feet deep. Or five hundred. It was impossible to tell.

"Nipper?" she asked again.

Samantha's heart raced as she thought about her

brother falling into the pit, lying helpless and in pain way down at the bottom. She listened for another groan, or a crash or a thump or some other terrible sound of an eight-year-old who had gone *splat*.

She held her breath and stared into the darkness.

"Sam, is that you?" her brother's voice echoed from a doorway on the right side of the room. "Come help me lift this chair. I think it's solid gold."

Samantha let out a sigh of relief. Then she began to inch carefully around the edge of the room. As she moved, she noticed that, unlike the temple above, which had a stone floor, this chamber was paved with red clay tiles. They were dirty and worn, and cracked with age.

Every few feet, a shiny metal panel stuck out from the wall, and each panel was held in place by a metal bracket. Between the panels, the walls were covered with drawings. They were strange—stranger than the ones in the Temple of Horus above. And there was a lot of writing. It was mysterious. It looked nothing like what she'd copied from "The Traveler and the Monkey King."

There were lots of pictures of skulls and of weird people waving swords. There were all kinds of fish and birds. One large drawing appeared to show a giant squid.

The images seemed out of place. Samantha shivered. Everything here looked creepy. There was something bad about this place.

Samantha reached the doorway, turned right, and stepped into a new room.

Light streamed in behind her from Dennis's collar, illuminating another chamber. It was bigger than the chamber with the pit in the center, and it was filled with fantastic objects. Everywhere she looked, the walls were covered with silver masks—creepy faces and skulls and animal heads. Ornate caskets and shimmering statues leaned against the walls. Baskets overflowing with coins and gems covered the floor.

Nipper was busy dragging a shiny chair toward the center of the room. The heavy scraping sound echoed as he tugged it, gouging out a trail of broken tiles and earth behind him. He was pulling it over to a pile of glistening silver skulls. Samantha could see spaces on the walls where Nipper had pried loose the masks. Dark soot trickled out of holes where the masks had been attached.

Nipper pushed the chair up against the mountain of objects and stopped. He adjusted some of the creepy silver faces that balanced on the pile.

Samantha didn't know what he was up to, but she was sure it wasn't good. "What are you doing?" she asked her brother nervously.

"This is my chance," he said. "So use your big brain to help me figure out how I can haul these things home."

"Your chance?" Samantha looked around the room.

She could see that he had removed the tops from several large urns. A wooden sarcophagus covered in mysterious writing and speckled with pearls rested in one corner. Her brother had pried off the lid and propped it against a nearby wall. A stream of crud was oozing around the casket from a large hole in the wall where he had pulled a mask free.

"Nipper!" Samantha shouted. "Have you lost your mind?"

"No, Sam. I lost my Yankees," he answered. "I'm going to sell this stuff so I can get my baseball team back."

As he spoke, something on his hand flashed in the

light. Nipper was wearing a large black-and-green ring on his finger. It was shaped like a scorpion and had two glittering green eyes. Samantha didn't need her fashion-expert big sister Buffy to know that they were emeralds. Enormous emeralds.

"Where did you get that thing?" she asked.

"I pulled it off the mummy in the box," he said, and pointed his thumb over his shoulder at the coffin. "It wasn't making him look fabulous, that's for sure. And I really need it so I can— Ouch!"

Nipper poked his thumb into his own eye.

For a moment, Samantha thought she saw the eyes on the scorpion ring glow.

Nipper crossed the room again and started to drag a heavy onyx table over to his treasure pile. It was covered in turquoise beads.

"I'll have enough money to buy a second baseball team," he said. "Maybe the Boston Red Sox. And you'll get rich, too. There can be two Scarlett Hydrangeas in our family."

He lost his grip and fell backward onto the floor. As he stood up, he smacked his forehead on the edge of the table.

The emerald scorpion eyes flashed. Samantha was sure this time.

"I know, Sam. It's an awesome magical ring and it's

cursed," said Nipper. "I started stumbling all over this place and banging into things way before you got here."

She watched him bend down to grab a small golden statue of a jackal.

"I'm just going to add a few more treasures to this pile and— *SAMMY!*"

CHAPTER TWENTY-TWO

EXCEPTIONALLY GROSS

Samantha hated being called Sammy. She liked Samantha or Sam, or even the occasional Mantha. The name Sammy, though, had always bothered her.

Three years ago, the Snoddgrass family had gotten a puppy. As a prank, Nipper convinced them to name it Sammy. For an entire summer, various family members would lean out a window and shout, "Sammy! Come here, Sammy. Good girl, Sammy!" several times a day. It drove Samantha crazy.

Samantha got revenge on her brother three months later. The night before school started, she filled in all of his permission slips using the first name "Pynchon." Nipper handed in the forms without noticing. For the entire school year, whenever a teacher, coach, or chaperone called out "Pynchon Spinner," the kids would shout, "Yes, sir!" or "Yes, ma'am!" And they'd give Nipper a pinch.

Nipper never called his sister Sammy again . . . until now.

The mummy from the coffin was standing upright, with both of its arms stretched out toward Nipper. It was seven feet tall, and it was a shambling mess. Putrid fingers poked through snarls of crusty linen strands. Mustard-colored soot leaked from the bandages that wrapped its face. It was the twenty-fifth-worst-smelling creature Nipper had ever encountered.

"Move away!" Samantha shouted as she jumped sideways and then dashed across the room.

"Wait, Mummy!" Nipper shouted up at the moldy figure. "I have money!" He reached into his pocket and held up the bill Uncle Paul had given him.

The mummy continued sliding forward. Just as it was about to reach him, its arms fell from their sockets. Then its head turned upward, rolled backward, and dropped from the shoulders.

"Yaahhh!" Nipper shrieked, letting go of his bill.

Samantha caught a glimpse of President Woodrow Wilson as the money fluttered into the air.

The mummy fell forward, lifeless, and was propelled past Nipper by the stream of crud that now sprayed from the hole in the wall behind the casket. Then the

wall started to crumble and the hole became wider. The slimy spray became stronger.

"Sam!" Nipper shouted, watching the bill flutter. "I lost my—"

With a sudden loud, belching sound, a jet of crud spewed forth, gushing from the opening in the wall. It knocked Nipper down and swept him up in a gooey brown tide.

"*Saaa-meeeeee!*" he screamed.

Samantha hugged the wall on the far side of the room. She looked all around, trying to think of a way to help her brother.

The filthy avalanche rumbled across the room, pushing aside the treasures and dragging Nipper along with it. His sunglasses fell off. Trapped in the sludge, he struggled to keep his face above the muck as it carried him out of the treasure room.

"*Ahh!*" Nipper screamed. "*Ahh-ack!*"

Something round and slimy slipped into his mouth. He pushed it around with his tongue. It might have been a big gem or one of the disintegrating mummy's eyeballs—he couldn't be sure. He spit it out as fast as he could.

He kept thrashing about in the sludge, but he couldn't get free as he slid through the doorway and into the round chamber.

Dennis looked up from his empty plastic bag and saw the approaching wall of dust, mud, mummy parts, screaming boy, and slimy goo. He scampered quickly along the curved wall and out through the doorway on the opposite side of the chamber.

The gushing, grimy river banked along the walls and swirled around the edges of the room like a giant toilet bowl flushing. Green and brown crud covered most of Nipper's face, and he could only see out of one eye. His desperate breath bubbled out of his nostrils and into the gooey muck.

In his heart he knew that if anyone ever wrote a book about his life, the title of this chapter would be "Exceptionally Gross."

He watched helplessly as the patterns on the ceiling spiraled above him. The raging river of sludge swirled faster and faster and began to drain into the pit in the center of the room—dragging Nipper toward it as well. Flat on his back, he flowed along with the muck. Unable to escape, he gritted his teeth and prepared to tumble into the awful darkness.

"Nipper!"

He heard his sister shout and squinted with his one clear eye.

Samantha was above him, leaning in from the wall. With one hand she hung on to one of the brackets that held the shiny metal panels. Her other hand gripped the umbrella by its handle high above her.

"Saaaam-meeeeee!" Nipper screamed.

She plunged the umbrella down toward his neck. The metal tip pierced his shirt collar and drove into the floor like a magic spear.

CHAPTER TWENTY-THREE

OPENING DAY

Rumbling and roaring, the cascade of crud washed over Nipper and poured into the black pit. He gurgled and thrashed as the muck streamed around him, but the umbrella tip through his collar pinned him to the clay-tiled floor.

The deep, dark pit swallowed it all. The grimy river slowed to a trickle. Then it was spent.

Samantha walked over to Nipper. Without saying anything, she yanked the umbrella from the floor. She reached out to help him up but stopped herself when she looked at his slime-covered hand, and arm, and body.

"That's okay, Sam," Nipper said. His shoes squished as he stood up on his own.

The room had dimmed when Dennis went through

the doorway opposite the treasure room. They followed the light and walked along the curved path.

Just before they passed through the doorway, Samantha tapped Nipper on the shoulder.

"These are yours, I believe," she said, holding out his sunglasses.

Both kids donned their shades at the same time and walked into the new room.

This rectangular chamber was lined with elaborate banners. Long sheets of fabric of different patterns and colors covered every space on every wall from floor to ceiling. Some were in solid colors, and some were striped. Several were covered in Egyptian-looking symbols. Others featured geometric patterns. Most of them were streaked with dust and cobwebs.

Lighting the room with his collar, Dennis shuffled around the chamber, sniffing at the floor.

Samantha and Nipper watched their dog move about. He sniffed his way over to a wide, dark shape on the floor and stopped. He stared at the floor and began to whimper softly.

"What's up, pug?" Nipper asked.

Dennis stopped whining and looked up at the kids. His nose was flecked with tiny orange dots.

"Dennis," said Samantha. "What did you find that— Oh my."

Dennis stood in the center of the wide black mark.

Something had been burning there recently, scorching the floor and leaving ashes and strange orange flecks. For several feet in all directions, the floor was covered with bright orange bits. Nervously, Samantha leaned forward and took a closer look at the floor.

There were blown-up pieces of orange shoes everywhere.

"I . . . was right," Nipper said softly. "Uncle Paul exploded."

When he'd said that weeks ago, Samantha had thought it was absurd. She had never even considered that Uncle Paul might really be dead. She was sure she was going to find him. She had never given up.

But there were blown-up flip-flops all around them.

Her brother was right. The silly officers were right.

Uncle Paul was really gone.

Samantha and Nipper stood in the center of the awful spot for a long time, staring at the floor. Neither of them had anything to say. Not even Nipper.

Dennis whined again and looked up at them.

Nipper reached out to pet the pug, but Dennis sniffed his hand several times and shrank back.

"I don't blame you," Nipper said.

"Hold on," said Samantha.

She reached over to the wall and pulled at one of the long banners that hung from high above. She held it out for her brother to use as a towel.

Nipper took the cloth and began to wipe away his coating of grime.

Samantha stood there, watching her brother.

As Nipper dried his hair, she looked over his shoulder and noticed something odd about the fabric behind him on the wall. Unlike the old, faded textile she had just handed him, this one was crisp and clean. It was a long blue flannel sheet printed with cows and horses. The faces on all the cows were printed upside down. The horses had five legs each.

She followed the pattern down to where the fabric touched the floor. In the lower-right corner, she eyed the all-too-familiar letter *S* curved around the letters *F* and *C*.

"Seattle Fabric Center," Samantha announced as she reached out and grabbed the sheet made of 90-percent-off misprinted flannel. She yanked it from the wall. It slid off the pole that ran along the ceiling and fell to the floor.

Nipper finished wiping his head and turned.

Both kids gazed at the newly revealed wall. It was bare stone from the floor to the ceiling, except for four large tiles that formed a square, about even with their faces. Each tile had a simple picture in its center.

"Waves, flames, moon, sun," said Samantha, naming the images on the tiles.

"What do you think, Sam?" Nipper asked. "Does that mean anything to you?"

She examined the tiles again.

"Water, fire, night, day," she said.

They both stared at the wall a while longer. Then Samantha took a step back and turned away.

She let out a big sigh. "I give up," she said sadly. "And if Uncle Paul's really gone, I'm not sure I care anymore."

She hung the umbrella on her shoulder. "Let's get

out of here. This place gives me the creeps," she said, and started heading out of the room.

But an arm popped up, blocking her path. It was Nipper's.

"Waitaminute, waitaminute, waitaminute!" he yelled.

Samantha stopped and turned around.

Nipper pointed at the picture of the sun.

"Uncle Paul told me not to miss opening day!" he shouted.

"So?" asked Samantha.

"So that's *day*," he said, and started tapping at the tile with his index finger.

There was a hollow click.

Nipper froze with a surprised look on his face. He yanked his hand away.

Slowly, the tile with the picture of the sun flipped open. Behind it was a space in the wall.

"See?" said Nipper triumphantly. "I didn't miss *opening day!*"

The space was about the size of a shoe box. Samantha peeked inside and saw a letter wedged at the back. She reached in and plucked it out.

She smiled.

"Wait," said Nipper. "How do you know that's meant for you?"

It was a single sheet of paper, folded in thirds and

sealed with a scratch-and-sniff sticker shaped like a strawberry.

Samantha rubbed the sticker and sniffed. Immediately she thought of Uncle Paul and his strawberry waffles, and all the mornings they'd spent together waiting for the bus, and all the afternoons they'd spent collecting things, and all the evenings they'd spent sharing stories, solving puzzles, and talking about amazing places around the world.

Then she unfolded the paper and read out loud.

"Dear Samantha,

When I found out about the umbrella, it was the beginning of an adventure . . . and a whole lot of trouble!

Those ninjas were using it to steal from everyone everywhere, so I knew I had to take it away from them.

I waited until it was the monkey's turn to carry around the Plans. Then I tricked him into competing against me in a hula hoop contest. I let the monkey win so I could swipe the umbrella while his arms were in the air and he was still twirling. Without the Plans, the RAIN were stuck in France and they got double mad—and triple smelly!

I started returning stuff that the ninjas stole, and I looked forward to a long life as an explorer. I spent my time traveling and trading and brought back some crazy things. But mostly I collected stories for you.

Then something went wrong. Somehow, the RAIN figured out where to find me. And when a bunch of them showed up in Seattle, I knew the best way to protect you was to go missing!

So I put on a pair of rubber boots and wore an inflatable raccoon just to make sure the ninjas would see me. I headed out of town hoping I'd lure them after me and keep our family safe.

I left that check for Buffy to keep all the money out of evil hands. I knew she would go on a great, grand shopping spree and spread the money in so many places it could never be recovered.

I gave the umbrella to you, Samantha, because I knew you'd discover the secret of the Plans. Those ninjas—just like a lot of people—don't understand that the world has always been full of special secrets and amazing adventures. Maybe you're the one who was meant to have the Plans all along.

If you're reading this letter, then something's

gone really, really wrong. But you've made it all the way here, so I know you've learned to take a closer look at things. Nothing can stop you from going anywhere you want to go.

You're the bravest and smartest person I've ever met, Samantha. I just wish I could be there to find out about your super-secret plans—the ones you'll come up with to set things right.

You have many places to go . . . and a lot to do!

—Uncle Paul"

CHAPTER TWENTY-FOUR

BUZZ!

At first Samantha wanted some more time to feel bad about losing Uncle Paul. But she'd already done enough power moping to last a lifetime. She rolled up the note and shoved it into her pocket.

"The RAIN is gonna fall hard now," she said. "Let's go, Nipper."

She looked over her shoulder.

"Nipper?"

He wasn't there.

"Ugh," she said, and marched back through the doorway to the chamber with the awful dark pit. Dennis was near the wall again, keeping a lookout for trouble or crackers. She continued along the wall, following the sounds of heavy objects being dragged across a muddy clay-tiled floor.

Nipper was back in the treasure room.

She hurried through the doorway. Then she stopped.

Samantha crossed her arms and watched as Nipper filled a bucket with sticks. They were made of different types of wood, and they all looked suspiciously like magic wands. He picked up a shiny gold ring with strange writing on it and a glistening pair of ruby-studded slippers. He tossed them both in the bucket and added it to a new stack of trinkets and treasures. Then he bent down and picked up a creepy-looking monkey's paw.

"Enough!" she shouted.

Nipper stopped and looked up at her. He let the paw fall on the floor.

"We're getting out of here now, and we're leaving all this stuff right where it is," she commanded.

Nipper started to protest, but she shoved him away from the treasure pile.

"Come with me *now*!"

Nipper stood where he was, frowning. Then he spoke very slowly.

"I . . . want . . . my . . . Yankees . . . back," he said. "What else can I do?"

"You could at least say thank you to me," said Samantha.

"Thank you?" he asked. *"Thank you?"*

"I saved you from a horrible, slimy death!" she shouted. "I think you should say thank you, and *merci*, and *arigatō*!" She grabbed his arm and began to pull him across the floor. "That's 'thank you' in Japanese," she added.

Nipper tried to pull away, but Samantha didn't let go. She dragged him out of the room and along the curved wall toward the mouth of the tunnel.

"Okay, okay," said Nipper. "I'm going."

Samantha let go of his arm.

"But as soon as we get back to Seattle I'm never speaking to you again," said Nipper. "Wherever you go, I'll head in the opposite direction and stay one hundred percent angry with you forever."

"That's fine with me," said Samantha. She looked Nipper straight in the eye and pointed at him. "Just don't forget to leave everything you've stolen from this tomb."

"Absolutely. I won't," said Nipper, covering his right hand with his left to hide the ring on his finger.

Samantha adjusted the umbrella on her shoulder, and watched to make sure Nipper and Dennis went first. They walked carefully around the room with the horrible pit and into the exit tunnel. One after another, they crawled out of the secret tomb, back up to the museum and the Temple of Horus.

They wound their way to the museum exit, across the pillar-lined courtyard, and back up the giant falcon's tail, across its back, and up and over the rim of the hat on the massive statue's head.

As they climbed through the secret hole, back down the ladder into the magtrain station, Nipper lost his grip and tumbled to the floor. As they walked down the ramp to reach the H-shaped magtrain car, he tripped on his shoelaces two separate times. Getting into the front bench, he bashed his funny bone on the side of his seat.

"Ouch!" he wailed, rubbing his arm.

Samantha glared at him. He put his arms close to his sides and gave her a weak smile.

She took her place in the middle seat, placed the Plans on the floor by her feet, sat Dennis on her lap, and pressed the button. Her hair stood up, and the tracks began to glow once more as the magtrain accelerated.

"You must really want that cursed thing," she called to him. "I can't believe you didn't put it back where you found it."

"I need it for something special," he said, shooting her a look over his shoulder. "And I won't let you boss me out of it."

As he turned to face the front of the speeding magtrain, a bug flew up his nose.

The scorpion's emerald eyes flashed brightly.

Samantha shook her head, while Dennis settled in comfortably. The car raced along swiftly but quietly through the tunnel.

Samantha noticed the soft buzzing sound again. It was definitely coming from Dennis, and it was really starting to irritate her. She inspected the pug's neck carefully. The noise wasn't coming from the Blinky Barker after all. It was coming from the dog collar—from a speck on the huge blue gem attached to its front. She squinted and looked even closer. It wasn't a speck; it was a tiny electronic chip, and it was glued to the stone's surface.

Suddenly everything made sense. "*That's* how the ninjas have been tracking us," Samantha said quietly. She yanked the gem free from Dennis's collar and raised her arm, about to toss the gem onto the tracks behind them. Then she stopped . . . and smiled.

"Nipper," she called. "Before we split up and always head in opposite directions and you stay one hundred percent angry with me forever, I want you to take this."

She held out the big blue gem.

Her brother turned around and looked at what Samantha held in her hand. Silent and scowling, he grabbed the gem.

He held up his other hand and showed Samantha that he was pulling the scorpion ring off his finger. He grunted and stuffed both the gem and the ring into his pocket. Then he turned away from her as the magtrain car sped onward to Seattle, the Emerald City.

Machu Picchu

Machu Picchu is an ancient abandoned city in the mountains of Peru.

It was built around the year 1450, and it served as a royal estate for the rulers of the Inca Empire. It had temples, houses, aqueducts, fortifications, and many terraces for farming.

Perched at 7,970 feet above sea level, it is surrounded by steep mountain peaks on three sides. This makes it hard to find and just as hard to reach.

No one is sure exactly when or why it was abandoned. It is often called the Lost City.

*　*　*

Enter Machu Picchu from the south, turn left, and head up the stairs from the main road until you come to a set of walls and terraces. Look for a large, flat slab of rock carved from a single boulder. There is a row of six holes drilled into it.

Many small pebbles will be scattered around the area. Gather six of them and drop one into each hole. As soon as you drop the last pebble, you will hear a sound like the crack of a whip, followed by a loud *twang*. It's a cable being pulled tight.

Climb over the low wall and turn to your right. Look carefully and you will see a chair dangling from above. It is painted the same color as the mountain and sky behind it, so you'll have to take a close look at things to spot it. There is room on the chair for two large people, or two children and a small animal, or one full-grown llama.

Once all passengers are ready, rock the chair until it slips off the brace and drops onto the giant cable. You will gain speed rapidly as you glide around the mountain and zoom down through the forest.

This is the fastest way to travel from Machu Picchu to Lima, Peru, about 250 miles away.

CHAPTER TWENTY-FIVE

100 PERCENT ANGRY FOREVER

Samantha, Nipper, and Dennis headed up and out of the magtrain station and back toward Thirteenth Avenue. They'd walked halfway down the block when Nipper stopped.

"Keep going," he told Samantha. He pointed in the direction of their house. "Don't come back for me. I'm one hundred percent angry with you forever." He stood there waiting for Samantha and Dennis to walk away.

Samantha didn't say anything. She walked quickly, and Dennis trotted along after her. As she neared their house, she broke into a run. She dashed down the driveway and through the side door to the kitchen. She headed straight through the living room. She passed her parents, sitting next to each other on the couch. Together, they were holding a big hardcover book with the word *Chinchillas* on the cover.

"Back so soon?" asked her mother. "I thought you went to a triple-feature movie party."

"The sun is still very bright outside," said her father. "The angle of incidence of the light rays is—"

"Sorry," said Samantha, cutting him off. "I have many places to go and a lot to do!"

She ran upstairs.

Dennis stopped and watched her go. Then he sniffed around the living room and headed back to the kitchen in search of crackers or waffles.

In her bedroom, Samantha picked up two quarters from the top of her desk. Then she walked over to the window.

Her bedroom faced the front of the house and had a wide view of Thirteenth Avenue. She could see Nipper at the far end of the block. He was still standing there with his arms crossed, as if to make sure she wasn't coming back.

Finally, she saw him turn and stomp off into the park.

Samantha headed back downstairs and into the kitchen. She grabbed the umbrella that was leaning against the wall, and went out the door.

Soon she was back at the edge of the park, standing in front of the ordinary-looking mailbox.

She grasped the handle and opened and closed the flap three times.

CHAPTER TWENTY-SIX

DANGERS ON A TRAIN

The plaza around the entrance to the Louvre is a magical place. Visitors can take in the sights and sounds of Paris. They can head into the giant glass pyramid or tour the museum's exterior. From the right location, they can catch a view of the river Seine in the distance. On most days, there is the smell of freshly baked bread.

Enthralled by all of these wonderful things, a person can easily miss a young girl doing something unusual amid the bustling, excited crowd.

Then again, some people don't care about that stuff at all. Some people hate Paris. They don't find the art and culture magical. They wish there were an easy way to sneak out of France and never come back.

Those are exactly the kind of people who'd notice an eleven-year-old girl standing in the center of the plaza on a sunny day, opening and closing a red umbrella.

Samantha didn't see anyone approaching. But when she sniffed the air, she took in the smell of French bread . . . and rancid garlic, gasoline, and four hundred pounds of used kitty litter.

She closed the umbrella once more and stomped on the ground four times, lifting her knee high in the air before each stomp. She wanted to make sure that anyone watching could see exactly what she did.

The tile beneath her dropped, lowering her into the station below.

Samantha walked along the ramp to the tracks without looking back and sat down in the center seat of the magtrain car.

Then she waited.

As soon as she caught a whiff of rotten eggs and window cleaner, she tapped the red oval button to start the motor.

The tracks beneath the train began to glow, and the car started moving.

Two black-shrouded ninjas leaped onto the bench in front of Samantha just as the car pulled away from the station.

She looked over her shoulder. Two more ninjas had taken the seats behind her. She recognized the smelly, bread crumb–covered man she had met on her first trip to Paris.

"Stupid girl," he said. "You showed us how to find the train. Now we're back in business." The dried pieces of gum that stuck to his face wiggled as he talked.

Samantha pretended not to hear him and turned forward again. She stayed seated, watching the yellow readout lights.

000004 MPH
000005 MPH
000012 MPH

"You must think you're pretty clever," he said from behind her. "Well, we have our little tricks, too."

000090 MPH
000220 MPH

"We're the ones who put the transmitter on the Hope Diamond," he said. "After we found out your weird uncle was in Seattle, it was easy to follow the signal to him."

000518 MPH

"And it was child's play to switch his flip-flops for a pair of exploding orange sandals."

002503 MPH

015130 MPH

"Pajama Paul?" he chuckled. "It was more like *Kablamma* Paul!"

The other three ninjas joined in laughing with him.

They all kept laughing, bathed in the glow from the tracks under the car. Samantha sat silently. They were about six minutes into the ride. The magtrain coasted onward.

"We're going to give you one last chance," said the voice behind her. "Give us your umbrella now and nobody else gets hurt.

"Except for that little brother of yours," he added. "He's so annoying. I'm going to find him and chop him up no matter what."

Samantha stood and turned around. The ninjas were standing with their swords drawn. Samantha drew her umbrella.

"What are you doing?" asked the crumb-gum man.

"This umbrella," she said. "I'm going to let . . . you . . . have it."

She raised her right arm and pointed the umbrella right at him.

"Oh no you don't!" the ninja shouted. He leaned backward, beyond the reach of the umbrella, and sheathed his sword. The other ninja stood still, waiting to see what he would do next.

Crumb-Gum put his right hand into a pocket in his black robe. He drew it out slowly and raised it high over his head. He held three silver shuriken, fanned out like playing cards.

As he whipped his hand forward, Samantha pressed the button at the base of the umbrella handle and the bright red octagon sprang open. One throwing star bounced off a spoke. The other two stars tore through the fabric and sailed past Samantha's head.

"Ouch!" a voice behind her shouted. "Watch where you fling those things."

Samantha closed the umbrella. She saw the two ninjas in the rear seat smile at something over her shoulder.

She waited until she could smell wet paint and pickle juice. Then she spun around and swung the umbrella like a right-handed power hitter for the New York Yankees.

Wham! She struck a ninja on the side of his head. Then she turned and swung the umbrella like a left-handed power hitter for the New York Yankees.

Wham! She connected with the other ninja in the front of the car.

Samantha bobbed and weaved. She dodged samurai swords and swatted at stink-bandits. Each time she struck a smelly arm or face with the umbrella, she could hear fabric tearing. Several small screws that held the spokes together popped out. She whacked Crumb-Gum twice on the bridge of his nose. The second time, the tip of the umbrella snapped off. It stuck to one of the pieces of gum on the ninja's face. Unable to see, he shook his head back and forth violently. Then he pulled the tip free and tossed it angrily over his shoulder.

Samantha lost track of the time, but she knew the magtrain was getting close to Seattle. She felt the car beginning to slow.

A grimy ninja hand reached over Samantha and grabbed the top of the umbrella.

"Gotcha!" the ninja blurted, and began to pull.

At the same time, Crumb-Gum swung at her again. She heard a snap as his sword sliced clear through the umbrella above the handle.

The ninja holding the umbrella lost his grip. Everyone froze and watched the tattered remains of the umbrella spiral over his head and onto the tracks in front of the car.

There was a loud crunch as the magtrain rolled over fabric and metal rods. The ninjas stared at Samantha as they cruised onward. There was nothing left of the umbrella but the long black plastic handle in her hands.

The car pulled into the station.

Samantha looked at the handle. She flung it at Crumb-Gum.

He ducked and it sailed over his head.

Samantha leaped from the car onto the platform. Without looking back, she raced to the main chamber. She stopped and waited. She listened to the ninjas climb out of the magtrain.

"There she is!" shouted Crumb-Gum.

Samantha bolted up the stairs and into daylight. She dashed toward her house. When she was halfway down Thirteenth Avenue, she stopped again and looked behind her.

The four ninjas emerged from the chamber beneath the raised mailbox. One of them pointed at her. Another pointed in the opposite direction. Samantha looked to see what he was pointing at.

The remaining twenty members of the Royal Academy of International Ninjas were marching into Volunteer Park.

CHAPTER TWENTY-SEVEN

THANK YOU FOR NOT JOKING

Nipper was furious at Samantha for making him leave all that treasure behind in the tomb. He couldn't buy his Yankees or any other baseball team, and he was really, really mad. For a while.

Nipper wasn't the kind of person who could stay 100 percent angry with anyone forever.

By the time he reached the center of the park, he was bored with being mad at his sister. He looked up at the art museum. The doors were propped open, and there was a noisy crowd inside. Some kind of event was under way.

Nipper reached into his pocket and took out the big blue gem. He tossed it in the air happily and caught it.

Then he skipped up the museum steps, excited to show it off to anyone willing to take a look.

His foot slipped and he stumbled as he neared the entrance, but he caught the handrail and kept his balance.

He patted the shape in his front pocket and kept going.

The lobby was packed from wall to wall with adults. A group of men and women were playing banjos and accordions. All of them had oversized fake mustaches and wore badges that said *Nasjonalmuseet.* Whatever that meant.

He noticed the words *Police du Louvre* on the lapels of two women in gray business suits.

Many people were dressed like famous works of art. Someone walked by inside a giant soup can. Another person wore a clown costume.

Nipper saw a huge banner draped above the windows on the back wall.

STARCH

STOLEN TREASURES AND ARTWORK RECOVERY

CONVENTION AND HOEDOWN

A pack of men and women wearing bowler hats and green T-shirts with pictures of llamas pushed past him on their way to the door. Nipper turned and saw the words *Seguridad de Machu Picchu* on their backs.

Then he spotted a trio of men in togas standing around a huge punch bowl. They were handing out drinks and frosted cookies shaped like statues.

As he headed to the snacks, Nipper passed a man and a woman talking. He glanced at their attendee badges. The man was from Wahoo, Nebraska. The woman was from Wagga Wagga, Australia.

"If there were cows in here, this would be a MOO-*seum*," said the man.

"Don't arrest that painting. It's been *framed*," said the woman.

Nipper scratched his head and thought about the jokes. He remembered seeing the two names on the arches in the magtrain station. It turned out neither Wagga Wagga nor Wahoo was particularly funny.

Then he looked down at his empty hands. He looked down at his feet and at the floor around him.

The big blue diamond was gone!

CHAPTER TWENTY-EIGHT

STARCH

Olivia Turtle stood in the lobby of the art museum, beaming with pride. It was the second day of STARCH. She loved meeting professionals from other countries and catching up on the latest gossip. It didn't bother her at all that her team came in a miserable last place in the trivia-quiz challenge. The art museum in Volunteer Park was her home turf, and she felt like royalty.

She noticed Pajama Paul's nephew moving anxiously through the crowd. He was darting around the lobby, looking under tables and chairs.

"What's the matter, soiled young man?" asked Olivia, tapping him on the shoulder.

"I had a diamond," he told her. "It was about this

big." He held up his hand and gestured with his thumb and index finger. "It was bright blue . . . and I lost it!"

Olivia didn't waste time wondering why a kid would have a gem that sounded a lot like the Hope Diamond. She reached for the bullhorn she kept stashed in the lobby's information kiosk.

"Attention, STARCH attendees," she barked. *"This is a code nine situation. Repeat. A code nine situation."*

Everyone in the lobby froze. The banjo players stopped strumming. Seconds later, the accordion players stopped squeezing. Dutifully, they all turned and listened to Olivia.

"A large gem has gone missing. It is a huge blue diamond the size of a walnut. This is not a test. Fan out, remain unobtrusive, and observe!"

CHAPTER TWENTY-NINE

THE STRANGE PARADE

Samantha hid behind a tree at the edge of Volunteer Park and watched the two dozen members of the RAIN as they huddled together.

She also noticed a woman in a bowler hat and a green T-shirt sitting on a park bench a few yards away, sniffing the air and eying them carefully.

Crumb-Gum addressed the group.

"First, we'll go in and take the diamond back," he said, pointing to the museum.

One of the ninjas was holding an electronic device with an antenna. He gave everyone in the group a thumbs-up.

"While we're there, check to see if there are any paintings worth stealing."

He made eye contact with several of the other ninjas and patted the rectangular shape on his back.

"There might be one or two guards inside," he added. "So chop first, ask questions . . . never."

They all drew their swords and tiptoed off to the museum.

Samantha waited until they'd disappeared through the front door. She figured Nipper would have lost the big blue gem by now. She headed after the RAIN, up the stairs and into the lobby.

Just as she had hoped, the museum was full of security guards. As soon as she stepped into the crowded lobby, she spotted Nipper. He was standing by the information kiosk with Olivia Turtle and two women in gray business suits. He was waving his arms and talking excitedly about something.

"That sounds very much like the Hope Diamond," Samantha heard one woman say in a thick French accent.

The other woman started to speak, but stopped suddenly. She sniffed and looked around.

The smell of stale cheese, rotten hot dogs, oil paint, ashtrays, and two hundred baby-changing tables filled the lobby.

The two women glanced at each other quickly.

"*Les Bandits Putrides!*" they both shouted.

"Watch out for the RAIN!" shouted Nipper.

Samantha smiled.

She had lured the twenty-four members of the Royal Academy of International Ninjas into a room with two hundred of the world's most dedicated security guards. The battle was over before it had really begun.

Most of the ninjas decided they were hopelessly outnumbered and dropped their swords. One got clobbered with a banjo.

As she watched a ninja banging his sword uselessly against the side of a guard's giant soup-can costume, Samantha thought about the entry in the *Encyclopedia Missilium*. Without the Plans, the RAIN was truly a mediocre outlaw gang!

Samantha heard a howl. She turned and saw the shortest ninja scampering around the room. He ripped off his ninja slippers and started leaping from statue to statue and swinging from light fixtures.

No one was able to catch the monkey until he stopped at the table with the frosted cookies. He picked up one that looked like Michelangelo's *David*. Then he dropped it and picked up one shaped like the Fountain of Neptune. He licked it three times, took a bite, and then put it back on the table. He used a foot to pick up another cookie, shaped liked *The Thinker* by Rodin, and began to rub it between two of his hairy toes.

Six security guards from Machu Picchu tackled him.

Crumb-Gum didn't give up. Samantha saw him slashing his samurai sword back and forth wildly. People began to panic. A crowd stampeded across the lobby, pushing Samantha backward toward the exit.

She peered over someone's shoulder and watched Crumb-Gum stop as he spotted Nipper.

"I'll make it easy for you to be on both sides of the Atlantic at the same time," he said, and charged. With both hands, he swung his sword down at Nipper's head.

Samantha pushed forward and burst from the crowd. She grabbed the ninja's sleeve, stopping the silver blade inches from Nipper's forehead. Then she pulled as hard as she could and yanked the ninja away from her brother.

Crumb-Gum's smelly black shirt came untucked and the heavy object hiding on his back came loose. A wood panel stuck out.

He jerked free and spun around, sending the board sailing through air. It arced up—and then down toward the punch bowl.

Olivia Turtle lunged forward. She pushed the clown out of the way, reached up, and snatched the tumbling object just before it splashed into the foamy red beverage.

She held it out before her, showing a full view of the painting. It was a portrait of a smiling woman.

"Whoa, Nelly!" shouted a visitor who was dressed like *The Scream* by Edvard Munch. "It's the *Mona Lisa*!"

Olivia cradled the painting gently in her arms, as if it were a newborn Italian baby from the 1500s.

Crumb-Gum whirled back around, looking for an escape route.

Samantha stood between him and the lobby exit. Hands at her sides, she blocked his path.

"Stop right there . . . please," she said. "That's English for *s'il vous plaît.*"

She raised her left hand, holding up a red umbrella.

"What?" the ninja screamed. "How?"

The umbrella in her hand was old and worn, and unlike her parents' black-handled umbrella—now lying crushed in the magtrain tunnel—it had a wooden handle.

It was the Super-Secret Plans.

"When? Who? Where?" asked the ninja.

"I've learned something very important," Samantha said. "I've learned to take a closer look at things."

The stink-bandit stepped toward her.

"And to watch out for stale bread, too!" she shouted, and swung at him with her other arm.

In her right hand she clutched a long, hard, three-day-old baguette she'd purchased outside the Louvre for fifty cents. She used it to smack him on the side of the head so hard that it dislodged several clumps

of dried gum from his forehead. He fell to the floor, knocked out cold.

Nipper ran to his sister. For a second, she thought he was going to give her a hug. Then he stopped. He smiled and put one hand on her shoulder lightly.

"*Shukraan,*" he said in perfect Arabic.

"You're welcome," said Samantha.

A few people congratulated a Norwegian woman in a big fake mustache for using her banjo as such an effective weapon. Many more people gathered around Olivia Turtle. They congratulated her for moving so quickly and saving the *Mona Lisa*.

"It's a good thing I recognized that famous painting right away," she announced. "I was able to do that because I heard so much about it from Pajama—"

She looked at Samantha and stopped herself.

"From Paul Spinner," Olivia finished.

Samantha stood with Nipper in the doorway and watched the STARCH conventioneers march the stinkbandits out of the museum and through the park. They continued down the street toward downtown Seattle.

Samantha knew that when they went back to school, Morgan Bogan Bogden-Loople would tell everyone that he'd seen the world's strangest parade. More than two hundred people walked down Thirteenth Avenue. Some were dressed like ninjas. Others were dressed like police officers. A few were dressed like famous works of art. A monkey screeched at everybody and swung from lamp to lamp all the way through the neighborhood. A woman in a uniform carried the *Mona Lisa*.

She was sure nobody would believe him.

CHAPTER THIRTY

THE GIFT

Samantha and Nipper walked around the water tower, out of the park, and past the mailbox. They were one house away from home when Nipper stopped suddenly. He put out his arm and blocked his sister.

"Ugh," she said as his arm whacked her in the belly. "What now?"

Nipper stood on tiptoe and peered down the Snodd-grass driveway.

"Wait right here," he said. "I really want you to see something."

Giggling, he skipped down the driveway.

He hopped over a hula hoop and continued toward Missy's house. He stepped on a strand of yarn lying on the ground and nearly wiped out, but he steadied himself and kept going.

Before Nipper could reach the side porch, Missy pushed open the screen door.

"So, it's you here again," she said, stepping outside.

Nipper stopped. He kept smiling as he looked up at her.

"Decent people always use the front steps," she told him. "This won't look good on your record."

He ignored this and cheerfully held out his hand. The black-and-green ring rested in his open palm.

"We went to London Bridge and I got you this present," he told her.

Missy looked at him suspiciously. Then she walked down three steps, letting the screen door slam behind her.

"Wait. What's that hole in your shirt?" she asked, pointing at his collar. "It looks like somebody else tried to stab you."

Nipper waited.

Missy looked down at the scorpion and gazed into its emerald eyes.

She grinned, exposing the large black space where one of her teeth was missing.

Slowly, she took the ring from Nipper and slid it onto the index finger of her left hand.

"Thanks. Now get out of here," she said briskly, and turned away.

Nipper took one careful step backward. He didn't slip or trip!

Quickly he spun around and dashed back to the sidewalk. He grabbed Samantha's arm and pulled her off the sidewalk and down into a bush.

"Ouch," she said. "What are you—"

"Shhhh," he whispered. "This is going to be great."

They crouched in the bush and waited.

Missy marched up the steps.

She didn't stumble.

She didn't fall backward down the stairs and land in poop.

She didn't accidentally bash her face against the house.

Missy grasped the handle of the screen door and paused. She looked back over her shoulder and shot a menacing glance in the general direction of Samantha and Nipper. They didn't think she could see them, but they both ducked a little closer to the ground.

"Jeremy Bernard Spinner," she called out. "I know you're hiding in that bush."

Then she turned back to the house and opened the screen door.

"Can we go home now?" whispered Samantha.

"Hold on," said Nipper. "Keep watching."

Missy didn't trip on her own shoelaces. An airsick owl didn't fall from the sky and smack her on the top of the head. A cement mixer didn't make a wrong turn down the driveway and accidentally pour cement all over her.

She disappeared into the house and the door swung shut behind her.

"This makes no sense at all!" Nipper wailed.

"She's Double-Triple-Super Evil," Samantha reminded him. "Maybe a cursed ring doesn't have any effect."

She could sense her brother's deep disappointment. He looked as if his head were going to explode.

"Don't worry," said Samantha. "I'm pretty sure we can figure out how all this crazy, mixed-up stuff fits together."

"You're starting to sound like Mom," said Nipper.

Samantha looped the umbrella strap over her shoulder. Then she held out her hand to help him up.

"Let's go home."

The Great Wall of China

The Great Wall of China is a series of walls, trenches, and fortifications along the northern border of historical China.

It was originally constructed between 250 and 200 BCE, incorporating many fortifications that were built hundreds of years earlier. It has been rebuilt many times over the centuries.

It is made of wood, dirt, bricks, and limestone. Some of the sections are massive constructions with towers and wide paved roads along the top. From end to end, the Great Wall is more than five thousand miles long.

The wall was built to protect Chinese empires from invasion. Today, it is a celebrated landmark. Almost everyone who visits northern China takes a trip to see the Great Wall.

* * *

Look for a section of the wall near Jinshanling, about eighty miles northeast of Beijing. You'll know that you're close to a secret entrance when you see a red trash can with a lid shaped like one of the Great Wall's towers.

Place your open hand against the wall on the huge gray stone that is a different color from all the others. Then withdraw your hand and wait until you hear the sound of a gong. (It will come from a speaker hidden in the trash can.)

If you lean against the stone, you'll be able to push it into the wall. Do not be startled by the sudden hissing sound of rushing air.

There is a secret staircase. As you walk down, the stone will slowly slide back into place behind you. You will find that it's impossible to exit the way you entered.

At the bottom of the stairs is a paved hallway that runs directly underneath the Great Wall. Rocket-powered bicycles have been stationed in plastic compartments every fifty miles along the path.

There are secret signs and markers hidden along the walls of this subterranean roadway. Be sure to bring a pair of invisible-ink-detecting glasses with you on your journey.

CHAPTER THIRTY-ONE

THE CURSE

Four weeks later, the Spinner family sat in the kitchen sharing amazing true facts and strawberry waffles. Samantha had completely stopped power moping, and her father had stepped up to become the new breakfast maker.

Samantha and her mother sat next to each other at the table.

Mrs. Spinner was busy filling out another Unexplained Vanishing Person Form. The last one had come back because someone had listed Uncle Paul's first name as "Uncle" and his last name as "Paul."

Samantha was studying her sketch from Edfu.

"I think that's Cleopatra's Needle," said Mrs. Spinner, looking over at the drawing.

"That seems awfully big for a needle," said Mr. Spinner, glancing down at the table. He held a plate piled high with fresh, hot waffles.

Samantha could never tell if her dad was brilliant or a grown-up version of her little brother. And was it a real needle, or something else? She looked up at her mother.

"What and where is Cleopatra's—"

"Hold that thought," said Mrs. Spinner. "I almost forgot." She took out a postcard. "This came in the mail yesterday, too."

The card featured several overlapping pictures, including the Statue of Liberty, Yankee Stadium, and the Empire State Building.

Samantha's mother read it out loud.

> "Dearest Mother, Father, Sammy,
> and Little Nipper,
>   I have wonderful news.
>   I spent most of the money and it looked like
> I was going to have to head back to dreary
> Seattle. Then, just in time, I got a call from the
> famous Broadway producer Horace Temple. He
> wants to cast me in his new musical show!
>   I hope you come and see my singing and
> dancing debut!

Kisses,

Scarlett Hydrangea

*PS: If you must write back about your boring
lives, be sure to send the letter to my new
address in New York City."*

Mr. Spinner shrugged. "I didn't think Buffy could sing *or* dance."

"Horace Temple?" asked Mrs. Spinner. "I've never heard of a famous producer named Horace Temple."

"It almost sounds like it could be an Egyptian name," said Mr. Spinner.

Samantha raised her eyebrows.

Nipper pretended to pay attention, but he was actually listening to the sports news blaring from the living room.

"Twenty-four games in a row!" a voice shouted.

The New York Yankees were setting a record . . . for the longest losing streak in the history of baseball.

"Some sports experts think that the Yankees are losing every game they play because of a terrible ancient curse," another announcer chimed in.

"How about that, old pal?" Nipper whispered to Dennis, who rested at his feet.

"Wruf!" the little dog barked.

Ten million candlepower's worth of pure white

light shot out from below the table. The intense rays reflected off windows, silverware, and appliances, filling the room with the glare of the X-27B lightbulb that Nipper and Samantha had absolutely forgotten to remove from Dennis's collar.

Mr. Spinner dropped the waffle plate and tried to shield his eyes. It fell to the floor with a crash, scattering waffles and strawberries everywhere.

"I recognize the color balance of that light," he said, bending down and reaching for the Blinky Barker.

Dennis bolted for a waffle . . . and seized it triumphantly, dashing out of the room and leaving a trail of syrup and powdered sugar.

Nipper and his parents chased the sticky pug. Samantha could hear them running from one brightly lit room to another, bumping into chairs and knocking over the coffee table. The sound of a lamp breaking came from upstairs.

Alone at last, Samantha glanced down at her notebook. She looked at the drawing of the mysterious obelisk.

"Horace Temple," she said. "*Horus* Temple?"

Something went *thump* and the kitchen table shook.

Samantha bent down and looked around. There was nothing to see.

Or was there?

She took a closer look and saw something she'd never

noticed before: three of the table legs were square and one was round. She put her hand near the top of the curved leg where it connected to the tabletop. A stream of air pulsed from a seam in the leg. She pushed gently on it and there was a click. When she pulled her hand away, a small curved door flipped open.

The leg was a pneumatic tube!

She pulled a small plastic cylinder from inside. She popped open the top with her thumb, and a pair of sunglasses dropped out onto the table.

They had silver frames. The lenses were purple and shaped like octagons. A small paper tag was tied to the bridge of the glasses. Samantha read the note.

Watch out for the SUN.
—Horace

Samantha smiled. It was Uncle Paul. He was alive, and Samantha was going to find him.

She stood up. Nipper was actually the very first person she wanted to tell about this discovery.

Then she heard several crashes overhead, and the sounds of her family chasing Dennis from room to room.

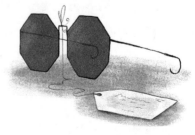

She sat back down and looked at her notebook.

The little black book had started out as a gloomy and depressing journal. Now it was becoming a guide to amazing places around the world, loaded with secret instructions. Samantha planned to add entries about the Eiffel Tower, the Louvre, and the other places she'd visited. And many, many other places she was going to visit.

Samantha flipped through the book until she found a blank page. Still smiling, she began to write.

There's a little bit of Nelly McPepper in all of us.

It's easy to believe that our hopes and dreams have been jacked up on a massive flat-bed truck and hauled away for good.

But take a closer look at things and you'll find there are possibilities everywhere.

All around, the world is waiting to reveal special secrets and amazing adventures.

We have many places to go . . . and a lot to do!

IT'S TOO BAD NIPPER DIDN'T KNOW ALL THESE
AMAZING TRUE FACTS

- Benjamin Franklin is on the $100 bill. President Woodrow Wilson appears on the *$100,000* bill. The Bureau of Engraving and Printing printed 42,000 of them from December 1934 to January 1935.

- The "Upside-Down Jenny" is a 1918 US postage stamp featuring a picture of an airplane. On one hundred of the stamps, the plane was accidentally printed upside down. This error has made them famous and prized by collectors. If you find one, it may be worth $500,000 or more.

- Action Comics #1 is the most valuable comic book in history. It was printed in 1938 and it includes the first appearance of Superman. A copy of it sold for $3,200,000.

- Honus Wagner, "The Flying Dutchman," played baseball from 1897 to 1917. He is on the world's rarest baseball card. Only 57 of them are known to exist. If you find one, it could be worth more than $5,000,000.

- The full value of the New York Yankees, including the baseball stadium and all the players' contracts, is about $2.5 billion.

WATCH OUT
FOR THE SUN!

Samantha and Nipper are hot on the trail of
unusual uncles, octagonal optics, and
alarming aromas in book two,

SAMANTHA
SPINNER
AND THE
SPECTACULAR SPECS

Coming
Spring 2019

WHOA, NELLY! THIS BOOK IS FULL OF

SUPER-SECRET SECRETS

The Secret Word Search: There's a word search hidden in the ID tags at the top-left corner of Samantha's journal. Stack them in order beginning with Section 01 on the top and see what happens. How many countries can you find?

Did you find the names of all thirteen countries in the secret word search? Now go back and take a closer look at things. The leftover letters will spell something important.

The Snoddgrass Code: There's a secret message hidden in everything Missy Snoddgrass says. Follow the numbers at the bottom of any page where she speaks. There's one digit for each of her words. The number tells you which letter to look at in the word. For example, the number 3 and the word *the* means the letter *E*.

The Magtrain MPH Message: There's another secret message, hidden in the magtrain speedometer. Each pair of bold numbers stands for a letter of the alphabet. 01 = A, 02 = B, etc. But . . . what could this possibly mean? Is it another clue? Is it a secret website? Do you have the foggiest idea?

The Umbrella/Hand Lens Enigma: Each chapter has umbrellas and hand lenses at the beginning. It turns out there's a point to them. *A point.* Get it?

Use these super-secret decoders to discover the message.

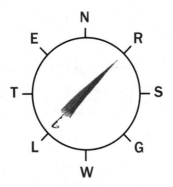

This is R, for example. (The handle is pointing to the right and the tip is pointing to R.)

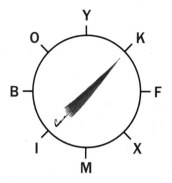

This is K. (The handle is pointing to the left and the tip is pointing to K.)

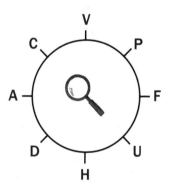

And this is U. (The handle is pointing to U.)

To learn more about all these puzzles, and a whole lot more secrets, go to samanthaspinner.com.

And if you can't get to a computer, or just want some help, keep reading!

SUPER-SECRET ANSWERS

Everyone needs a little help sometimes!
Here are the answers to the puzzles hidden
in this book.

THE SUPER-SECRET WORD SEARCH

The Puzzle:

Section	Detail									
01		I	M	I	F	R	A	N	C	E	S
02		T	M	O	R	O	C	C	O	G	T
03		A	S	Y	J	A	P	A	N	R	H
04		L	I	N	D	I	A	K	N	E	A
05		Y	O	W	C	H	I	N	A	E	I
06		I	R	A	N	S	A	B	O	C	L
07		M	E	X	I	C	O	U	T	E	A
08		T	Z	I	M	B	A	B	W	E	N
09		H	E	S	P	A	I	N	U	M	D
10		B	R	E	P	E	R	U	L	L	A

There are thirteen countries hidden in the puzzle.

The leftover letters spell this message:

The Answer:

MISSY KNOWS ABOUT THE UMBRELLA

THE SNODDGRASS CODE

The Puzzle:

At the bottom of any page where Missy speaks, you will find a row of numbers. Each number signifies which letter in each of Missy's words to keep.

For example, when Missy says: **"I know all about that,"** and **"Impressive."** The numbers at the bottom of the page are: **0005250000000005.** Each digit coincides with a word Missy says. The number refers to the position of the letter in that word to use to solve the puzzle. **5** means the fifth letter of the word. **0** means no letter. Thus, the hidden word in this example is **T-H-E.**

The Answer:

The complete message is:
THERE IS A SECRET WEBSITE
SNODDGRASS DOT COM

THE PASSWORD IS HULA HOOP

THE MAGTRAIN MPH MESSAGE

The MPH readout on the magtrain conceals a secret message, too! All of the pairs of digits that appear in bold represent letters according to their alphanumeric value.

01 = A, 02 = B, 03 = C, etc. This is sometimes known as the A1Z26 Cipher.

The complete Magtrain MPH Message is:

03	C	04	D
08	H	05	E
09	I	12	L
14	N	09	I
03	C	22	V
08	H	05	E
09	I	18	R
12	L	25	Y
12	L	03	C
01	A	15	O
		13	M

CHINCHILLADELIVERYCOM
(Go check it out!)

THE UMBRELLA/HAND LENS ENIGMA

The Puzzle:

At the beginning of each chapter you will see small illustrations of umbrellas and hand lenses.

Depending on which way each one is oriented and which way the umbrella handles are pointed, each drawing secretly represents a letter. (Hint: You need to use the decoder wheels on pages 236 and 237.)

Did you get it?

The Answer:

NELLY MCPEPPER WORE WHITE
BECAUSE IT WAS HER KARATE UNIFORM
SHE IS A MARTIAL ARTS MASTER

ACKNOWLEDGMENTS

This book exists because of three people.

Eva Ginns. You jump-started this story. You introduced me to Scarlett Hydrangea and Nelly McPepper. We haven't seen the last of each other.

Kevin O'Connor. Agent, advisor, and creative co-conspirator. What would this book be without you? Half as successful and one-third as good, that's what.

Krista Marino. At first I thought you were like Orson Welles in *The Muppet Movie,* making things happen. It turns out you're like Sherlock Holmes or Cousin Vinny. Nothing escapes you. Also, I suspect you might actually be a Spinner.

Then there's **Michael Artin, Dr. Carole Karp, Alex Alben, Courtney Nguyen, Darren Cahr, Wendy Bronfin,** and **Jonathan Maier.** You all deserve strawberry waffles.

As a writer, I owe a debt to the works of **Louis Sachar, James Morrow,** and **Sebastian Wreford.**

Thanks to **Sheldon Ginns** and **Jonathan Ginns** for sharing your love of art, architecture, and exploration.

And here's a big thanks to you readers who are taking a closer look at things. How many people read acknowledgments? If you've made it all the way here, then you deserve to know that this story has many more secrets. See you online!

ABOUT THE AUTHOR

Russell Ginns is a writer and game designer who specializes in puzzles, songs, and smart fun. He's worked on projects for Sesame Street, Nintendo, NASA, UNICEF, and Hooked on Phonics. He once had a poem published on the back of an Alpha Bits cereal box. Russell lives and writes in Washington, DC. To learn more about him, visit samanthaspinner.com.

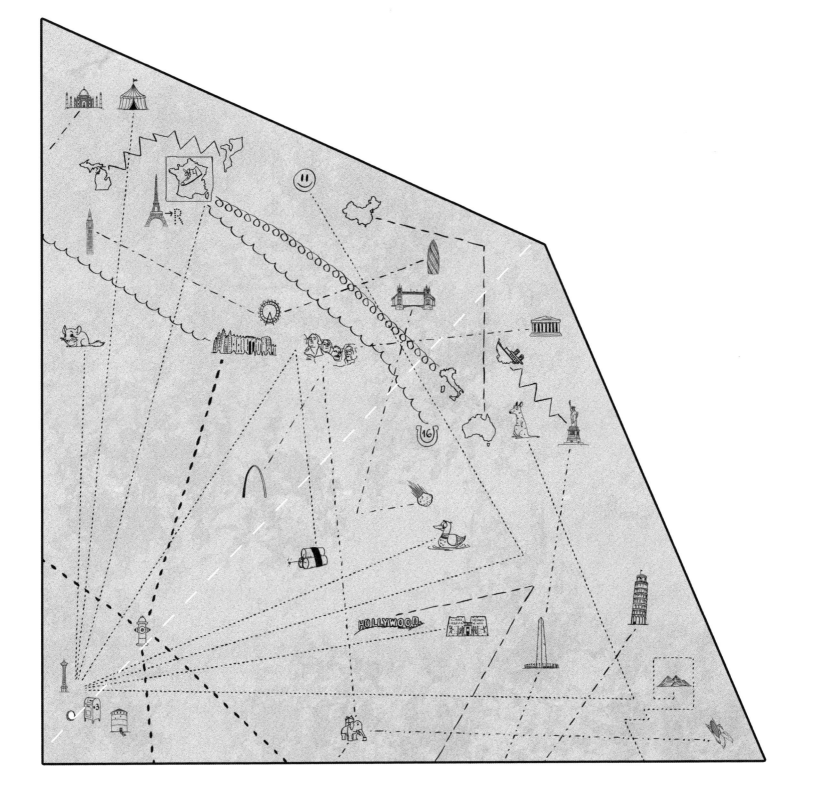